Haycox, Ernest
Secret river.

Secret River

Secret River

Ernest Haycox

Thorndike Press • Chivers Press
Thorndike, Maine USA   Bath, Avon, England

This Large Print edition is published by Thorndike Press, USA and by Chivers Press, England.

Published in 1994 in the U.S. by arrangement with the Golden West Literary Agency.

Published in 1995 in the U.K. by arrangement with the Golden West Literary Agency.

U.S.	Hardcover	0-7862-0254-8	(Western Series Edition)
U.K.	Hardcover	0-7451-2627-8	(Chivers Large Print)
U.K.	Softcover	0-7451-2633-2	(Camden Large Print)

Originally published in SHORT STORIES magazine.

The text of this Large Print edition is unabridged.
Other aspects of the book may vary from the original edition.

Set in 16 pt. News Plantin. 16.95

Printed in Great Britain on acid-free paper.

British Library Cataloguing in Publication Data available

Library of Congress Cataloging in Publication Data

Haycox, Ernest, 1899–1950.
Secret river / Ernest Haycox.
p. cm.
ISBN 0-7862-0254-8 (alk. paper : lg. print)
1. Large type books. I. Title.
[PS3515.A9327S4 1994]
813′.52—dc20 94-12081

Secret River

Chapter 1

According to Springtime Povy, who held original ideas on a number of subjects, the Lord had created the West because He very well knew a special and superior brand of mortal known as the cowboy would one day inhabit it. And then Springtime, combing down his sad looking mustache with thumb and forefinger, went on to amplify and embroider. The West, he asseverated, measured farther from top to bottom than any other known region, and that was to give the cowboy ample space in which to rise when he mounted some wall-eyed bronc that didn't nowise aim to stay on the ground. Furthermore, the West was made broad from corner to corner to prevent the cowboy's expanding thoughts from being cramped or imprisoned. Spring and fall were to give him an idea of how the sweet by-and-by would be like; while winter and summer were meant to haze a portion of the false pride and orneriness from his system.

When it was pointed out by a carping bunkhouse realist that other sections of the country likewise had hot and cold weather, Springtime built himself a cigarette and thus amalgamated the basic credos of his life. "Yeah, that may be right. But they ain't no heat spells like out here, nor any blizzards as bad. Now why do you reckon it was made thataway? Jes' because the cowboy is a wilder, tougher, stubborner animal than the lily-fingered pencil pusher back East, and the Lord knowed it'd take more severe conditions to haze him to a proper state of mind."

At about this point Springtime found he hadn't laid the proper foundation for his thesis. There was a regrettable skepticism pervading his audience, and since he was nothing if not practical he descended to a more prosaic level. "Well, mebbe I'm wasting the fruits of my mind on you misbegotten sheep-eaters. I thought you could think, which is my mistake. But here — how far is it to town?"

It was allowed, by one of the more substantial members of the bunkhouse, that twenty linear miles lay athwart Roan Horse and the ranch gate.

Springtime seized upon the fact with satisfaction. "Now why do you think it's that far? Think it was jes' an accident? No, sirree, bob. They ain't no accidents in this world. Them twenty miles was put there so's a Rocking Chair man could leave Roan Horse comf'tably illuminated and reach home sober. It if was any less distance he'd prob'ly get here in no fit shape for work, which would be very sad. Which illustrates how Providence takes care of the cowboy. Answer that, you limp-footed pedestrians."

There was no answer. Nothing but awe was visible upon the countenances of the bunkhouse gang. Or at least that was the expression Springtime thought he saw. He rose with the air of one who had spread manna before unappreciative ingrates and went inside to prepare himself for bed. The operation was simple and strictly followed range etiquette governing the negligee: he removed his hat, he removed his spurs and he rolled himself neatly into a blanket. But before dropping off to sonorous lumber he heard the reaction to his metaphysical deductions.

A foot scraped, a match flared and somebody murmured softly, "Ain't it hell?"

Springtime should have known whereof he spoke, for he had traversed that twenty miles many a time and, on the particular occasion this relation commences, he was covering the same territory once again, homeward bound from Roan Horse in a condition he himself would have described as "comfortably tight, but not too giddy."

It was going on toward sunset of a day in early spring. Borne up in the thin, sparkling air was the odor of sage and of wet earth steaming under the year's first hot sun. The creeks were bank full, the dry washes no longer dry, and on the high peaks could be seen black patches where a day before had been a solid mantle of snow. On the bench the bunch grass was turning green, while along the bottom the cottonwoods and alders had lost their sere and desolate appearance.

To a veteran like Springtime it should have reminded him that the years were beginning to roll along too fast; it should have reminded him also that they would presently be lining out on the spring roundup — which was no longer the gay time it once had been when he was a young fellow and thought nothing of eighteen hours straight in the saddle.

But no somber thoughts were in Springtime's head. The vernal impulses moved him this day as they moved all other animate things. The sap was running, a warm chinook blew out of the west and the sky was bluer than it had been for a half a year. It was good to be alive and to know the rheumatism had departed until the following wet season. Nor was this all; he had absorbed his pay check in good cheer at the Double O in Roan Horse and to start the year off properly had decked himself out in a pair of new boots, new gloves and a new bandanna, all of which bore the mark of the New York Mercantile Emporium (M. Fishbein, Prop.).

In his hip pocket was a carefully wrapped bottle of Frazer's Elixir of Seasons, a patent medicine which Springtime drank religiously at the break of the cold weather, full in the faith that it thinned his blood and otherwise toned him up. So he rode at peace, with an expansive feeling of good will toward all things great and small; ready to forgive his harshest critics. At intervals he struck his chest and said "whoooosh," in a rolling, lyric voice, looking with great interest at a particular landmark on his left flank.

"I'm getting sober, all right," he murmured. "That pinnacle was triplets a minute ago. Now it's twins. Well, I guess I'll be cured in another half hour. Whoosh."

Not being quite ready to hit for the ranch, he veered toward the bench, forded a newly made creek and climbed to higher ground.

Strange to say, notwithstanding the mellow kindliness bubbling inside him, his face presented a sad, austere expression to the world at large. In this respect Springtime was unfortunate. Mother Nature, in fashioning him, had done something to his cheek muscles, had left them stiff and unpliant. Springtime had never been known to laugh; nor had anyone seen anger upon him. He rode through the world, a lean, thin-chested man with hard squinting eyes, dangling, rawhide arms, and a pair of legs bowed beyond the power of description. Yet, in spite of his wooden face, Springtime had his humorous moments and his volcanic moments; the Rocking Chair boys could tell these moments by the drawl and grate of his voice.

Springtime said "whooosh" again and spoke aggrievedly to his pony. "It sure seems to me the Double O is putting out mighty poor liquor these days. Was a time when a pay check would furnish me with illumination enough to last right up to the ranch gate. Hell, I'm almost sober and not more'n half home. . . . Hey, what's that?"

Horse and rider stopped on the backbone of a ridge. Below, a stream sparkled under the last of the day's sun and the alders showed a verdant green. But in the foreground was the object of Springtime's attention; it was a cow, a brindle cow with her head lowered, bawling toward the four corners of the compass. She was not more than fifty yards off, and Springtime could plainly see her udder swollen with milk.

The sight of her seemed to sober Springtime. He straightened a little in the saddle and for a moment watched her. "It may be a natural error," he mused, "and again it may be a man-made bereavement. Push on, pony."

He struck for the creek bottom, circled the trees and without warning came upon another cow with a distended udder and a bawling voice. Springtime, alert and wary, started up the side of a hill, sweeping the land as he went. He was a good half hour in making the climb and by the time he had reached the top the sun had fallen into the west, leaving the world a mass of rose and purple shadows. Down on the other side of the hill flowed Secret River, showing darkly in the advancing twilight; a river that twisted and turned and doubled back in the bottom, forming miniature islands and dwarf peninsulas. At present it surged along with its snow water, but in another month or two it would be a sluggish rivulet. No matter. Springtime had spent his life in this country and he knew Secret River; he knew its moods and he knew the stories connected with it. Always it seemed a little shaded, somewhat sinister. No river in the county had as many treacherous fords; none could boast of a blacker history.

Springtime, running his glance back and forth, could have recalled many a manhunt along the stream if he had been in a reminiscent mood. But he wasn't. He had spied something dark on the ground, down in a little pocket of the hillside. He rode along and bent in the saddle; presently he circled around it, his half-closed eyes reading sign. In the end, he turned his horse to the summit and spent a moment staring into the distance. Out of sight, beyond the bend, was the Streeter outfit.

Springtime shook his fist in that direction and spoke briefly to his horse. "Travel now."

It was dark when Springtime reached the home ranch. The boys were sitting in front of the bunkhouse and as he rode toward them the comment rose in the balmy air, humorous and slightly ribald.

"Here's the vet'ran back from the battle. Light, Springtime and tell us another of them goshawful lies."

"Oh slap my wrist Algy. What's them duflickers he's a-wearing on his hands?"

Somebody tapped the steps and announced,

"Frazer's Elixir of the Seasons," whereupon the crowd gravely took up the chorus.

"This remedy guaranteed to cure asthma, dandruff, ear trouble, heart leakage, tuberculosis and allied ills. Taken externally it is a wonderful shaving lotion. Taken internally it is nature's own remedy. No ailing person can afford to be without Frazer's Elixir. Handy alike for gunshot wounds and goitre. Price two dollars the bottle in all drug and hardware stores. Civilization's greatest discovery."

Springtime ordinarily would have halted and blasted them with a few picked words. This time he went on, leaving the comment to trail and evaporate. Bringing up at the porch of the big house, he solemnly surveyed the three occupants thereon, seeming to wait for a greeting. Old Jim Bolles chewed on his cigar and said nothing. The schoolmistress ignored him. But young Jim Bolles leaned a little forward.

"Well, Springtime?" he said.

"Somebody," announced Springtime in a brittle voice, "is a-getting artistic with the running iron again. I found three-four cows bellering for their calves. And up in a hollow they was marks of a leetle branding fire." He looked again at the schoolmistress, and it seemed some kind of emotion tried to break through the stiff barrier on his face. But the girl stared deliberately over his head and he turned back toward the corrals.

The schoolmistress clucked her tongue, but young Jim was paying no attention to her. Father and son were exchanging glances in the semidarkness. The old man brought a sledge-hammer fist down on the porch railing. "They're declaring war on me, eh? Well, by Godfrey, I'll singe 'em! I'll break up that snake nest!"

Young Jim's face was grim; he shook his head in a wistful, unhappy manner. "I guess so. I guess it's got to be. Another range war."

Chapter 2

The schoolmistress, whose name was Evelyn Fleming, straightened in her chair and put a hand to her mouth. She was very young and very pretty in a pert, self-confident way, with a pair of flashing eyes and a face upon which emotions were continually passing. She had come from the East for the adventure of it and, after the fashion of the country, was virtually a guest of the Bolles' house while she taught at the prairie school two miles away. But the West had deceived her with its broad and smiling countenance. The romance and the picturesqueness of it did not immediately envelop her and she somehow failed to see the vital, primeval immensity of the terrific winters or the blazing heat of the summers. She was almost too clever, too quick at passing judgments, too prone to judge these people and this land after the standards of the East. And, with the exception of young Jim Bolles, her judgments were not complimentary. For that reason, perhaps, she had never discovered that beneath the slow-moving, kindly-speaking West there was a perpetual play of forces; she had never understood why the men of the Rocking Chair studied so carefully all the insignificant signs on the ground and in the air, nor why both old and young Jim seemed to be forever watchful when they were abroad. So this announcement fell on her ears like a bolt of thunder.

"War!" she cried. "My heavens! War with whom? Are you men fooling with me?"

Old Jim, after the fashion of his generation, was quick to cover up the trouble. His white head bobbed in the shadow. "Oh, Springtime is always bringing in sad news and he gets me riled. I'm an old fool, Miss Evelyn. Always shooting off my mouth. It's nothing to worry your pretty head about." He looked toward his son and got up. "I guess I better do a little figuring if I expect to keep from being foreclosed. Never buy a cattle ranch, ma'am. It's what give me gray hairs."

"I'm going to bed," she announced, likewise rising. "I'm terribly disappointed. For once I thought something exciting would happen around here."

Young Jim waited until she had disappeared

upstairs before turning toward his father's office. He shook his head and when he faced his father across the yellow lamplight he was frowning. Old Jim stood in a corner, waiting for his son, lines of anger cut deeply on his blocky, pugnacious cheeks. But he had time for one grim pleasantry.

"What's the matter with you, Jim? When I was your age I'da proposed to her, married her, and had a family raised by now. You're slow. Can't you see the gal's waiting to be asked?"

Young Jim flushed, saying nothing. The old man grunted. "You know best when the time's right. Now, by Godfrey, we got to singe the cat's whiskers. I've had enough stock rustled off me. Seventeen head of horses this winter and the Lord only knows how much beef. I wonder if them Streeters think I'm losing my grip?" He ended by smashing his fist down on the table. "I'll exterminate every damn Streeter on Secret River. I'll burn their houses down and erase every cussed thing they ever built. There won't be no more vermin breeding in this country when I'm through."

Young Jim said quietly, "We've got to have more proof, Dad. And I don't believe all of the Streeters are bad."

Old Jim flung up his grizzled head and

stared at his son. The two of them made a splendid show of physical strength as they stood across from each other. Each of them had the generous features of their tribe — the heavy chin and nose, the high cheek bones and the deep eye sockets from which came the characteristic straightforward, penetrating glance of the family. Here the resemblance ceased. Old Jim had been raised with a generation of grim, heavy-handed fighters who had pioneered and made their own laws, a generation that never would have a duplicate in cattle land. He had been a roistering, dangerous man, hard of heart toward his enemies but generous without stint toward his friends. His own hardships he had laughed at and consequently was callous to the sufferings of others. Now, with the frost on his head and his muscles overladen with fat, he was lord of his domain, a bluff, choleric man, proud of his power and ruthless toward anyone infringing on his rights.

Young Jim was half a head taller than his father, broader of shoulder and trimmed down from constant riding and work. Springtime had told the bunkhouse one day that young Jim was a better man than old Jim had ever been. "He's got a better head on him and he understands more about the other guy — sort of sympathizes with the under dog. As for shooting — he's the best in this here county, but he'd rather use his fists than a gun. When he goes into an argument, he don't like to leave any corpses behind."

Whereas old Jim's temper once caused him to roar in glee one moment and thunder his rage the next, young Jim rode on an even keel. He smiled seldom and he looked upon the world with sober, quizzical eyes.

"All the Streeters ain't bad?" shouted old Jim. "What moonshine you been drinking, son? That ain't like you at all. Listen, when a snake bites a man, he don't go around thinking mebbe it was just one snake that was vicious. No. He goes out and kills all snakes. Which applies to the Streeters. Never a Streeter I knew in twenty years was any good. I'm about to wipe the breed off the range."

"You've got to have more proof," said young Jim. The light gathered in pools around his eyes and the old man, looking at his son, was baffled.

"It's a curious way you got, Jim. I can't seem to read you no more. Well, I've got a man at the Portland stockyards and he's sending me proof a-plenty. And mebbe the Cattlemen's Association has got a word to say by and by. Yes, we'll be getting proof enough. Don't you worry. Your conscience won't bother you none when all the cards are on the table."

Young Jim moved restlessly around the room and came to a stand beyond the rays of the lamp. "It'll be a fight. I see everything smoking up that way. What's the matter with the due course of law in this county anyway? Hasn't the sheriff got guts enough to go in there and take those fellows? Why should there be a necktie party?"

"If you think any Streeter would submit peaceably to arrest you ain't read 'em right," said old Jim shrewdly.

"Maybe so," agreed his son. "Even at that, I guess you old fellows aren't so anxious to do it peaceably."

"Correct," said the old man. He threw back his head and chuckled, his massive body shaking with amusement. "You know the old-timers, don't you? It ain't pure bloodthirstiness either, boy. We learnt our poker in a tough game. What will the law do? Nothing. There's too many lawyers nowadays with their tongues oiled and hung in the middle."

Young Jim moved back to the light, squaring his shoulders. "Well, when the time comes I'll have to declare myself."

The elder's face wreathed itself in heavy lines. "This is as much your ranch now as it is mine. If a man won't fight for his property he ain't of much account."

"I'll fight my own way," declared young Jim. "I'm not going to go into a bust of shooting just because you old ducks want a little fun."

"That's your final word, eh?" growled old Jim, wrinkling his nose.

Young Jim hesitated. He stared somberly at the lamp and his face seemed at the moment gaunt and careworn. "I don't know, Dad, whether it is or not. A man can't get away from his own flesh and blood. We've got to keep the range clear, that's plain, too. I'll stay peaceable as long as I can. If something happens to shove me into this scrap, then I'll do as much fighting as the rest of you. But I don't want to be shoved into it, hear?"

"I wish I could read you, boy," said the elder wistfully. "You ain't yellow. I've seen you lick too many men to think that."

Young Jim shook his head and went out of the office. Presently he was riding away in the dark, the old man watching him go and wondering what he was about. From an upstairs window the schoolmistress likewise watched him; but being entirely a woman, she guessed whither young Jim was bound. She had seen him ride in the direction too often not to surmise what attraction pulled him away. And since her own heart was set on having young Jim, she flung herself down on the bed and spent a bitter hour.

Young Jim, once out of sight of the ranch, rode rapidly west and north until the trail crossed a creek. Here he struck up along a ridge and gave his horse a loose rein, riding as he best liked to ride — glad to be alone in a world cloaked alike with peace and with mystery. No moon sailed aloft, but the velvet, opaque universe was studded with countless diamond bright star points. Out of the darkness came the rustling rhythm of the small creatures of the earth and the sighing of the night wind through the occasional pines. Young Jim, relaxed in the saddle, felt the immensity of the heavens and his own insignificance. It should have been a depressing thought, yet it always served to dwarf his troubles; he could never ride abroad like this without catching hold, for a brief second, at the thought of infinity, and it always cleared his mind of the turbulence and the uncertainty of the day's work.

He came to the summit and angled down, seeing of a sudden the long, wavering beam of a light. Secret River was down there — and the Streeter ranch. Presently he was in a meadow, across which stretched a fence.

He could not see the fence, but the horse came to a stop and young Jim got down and whipped the top strand with his glove, softly. Near by sounded the half whispered reply of a woman.

"Jim? Stay there. I think Jere's along the river bank watching for someone." A foot struck a rock and a hand fell lightly on the man's shoulder. He took the hand eagerly. When he spoke it was in a rough, almost angry manner.

"When is all this going to end, Nan? Some of these days they'll catch on and then that fine brother of yours will use the horsewhip on you. Lord, it puts me at the end of my rope to think of it."

"Hush, Jim. It's too wonderful tonight for you to bring up all the unpleasant things. Look, there's our star again. I like to watch for it — but how can people be so foolish as to think the stars have any concern with this dusty troublesome old earth?"

"I guess we're all kind of foolish, honey. Else why should we be going around like chickens minus heads? Sit down there a minute." He crouched on the ground; a match burst like a bomb and a small ray of light shot up from his cupped palm, illumining her face.

It was a clear, oval face with a broad

forehead and a mass of black hair that seemed to absorb the light. She was seated on a log, her arms propped out and bringing into relief the sturdy lines of her shoulder, the fine, supple carriage of her body. Gray eyes widened and instantly she had reached forward and covered his palms. "You mustn't do that, Jim! If they caught you, they'd kill you! Something's in the air tonight. Everybody's in ugly temper."

"There's only one Streeter I'm afraid of," said Jim.

"Who?"

"You, ma'am. I'm afraid you'll stick with them too long. When are you going to let me take care of you, anyway? You're living in a den of thieves."

"They're my folks, Jim. I've got no others."

"Well, I'll supply you with a new set, pronto."

"Jim, I've got to stay! I'm the only woman in that house. Jere's children can't be left with the men. Oh, you're going to say I ought to bring them off with me. Jere would never stop then until he'd ambushed you. I've lived with Jere long enough to know his temper."

"Is that the only thing to hold you back?"

She was silent for a time. Her hand gripped

young Jim's fist. "No-o. I can't help being a Streeter. I know what the county thinks of the Streeter men. All bad — always have been bad. But they raised me and I owe them something for that. I guess I must have a little Streeter clannishness in me. Don't you think I haven't argued with Dad and Jere about going straight? They just laugh at me until I go too far. Then they begin to throw things. No, it'll just have to be this way until — "

He leaned forward and the girl felt the rising eagerness in him. "Until what?"

"I guess 'until' means always, Jim."

"No, it won't be that long." He was on the point of saying more, but checked himself. They had long ago made a bargain on that point; neither was to give away the plans of their families. But the girl knew what he had omitted.

"It's coming, then? The fight? They'll drive the Streeters out. Are you going to be with the crowd?"

"Lord, Nan, I — "

She stopped him, a cool hand across his mouth. "You will be, Jim. You have always been loyal. That's why I love you. But — I don't fit in. A Streeter and a Bolles? It doesn't even sound right. You're like all men — think marriage erases all these difficulties.

Jim, you had better please your dad and take the schoolmistress."

"I'm damned if I ever will," said young Jim flatly.

Her answer seemed to come from a great distance. "Well, it's good to hear you say that. Hark!"

Water splashed not far away and a figure passed across the light from the house. The girl's lips brushed his cheek, saying, "Stay here until I'm gone. Bless you, Jim. Don't take the same road home."

She was gone. Young Jim squatted by the fence a drawn-out twenty minutes. She should have passed across that light, too, in her trail to the house, but she didn't. As long as they had kept this secret meeting spot he had never seen her figure in the shadow, never known where she was until she called to him from the fence. There was something uncanny about the Streeter ranch; in twenty years no man had ever trailed a Streeter to his door.

Young Jim drew a breath of relief. She had reached the house safely, for a light appeared briefly at an upper window and a shade was drawn down. That was the signal he had waited for. Leading his horse along the side of the ridge, he fell away from his old path and followed the river's edge a quarter mile. Then mounting he pushed upward and across the ridge toward home, depressed and foreboding.

The old truce between the Streeters and the responsible cattle men of the county was about to be broken. He knew that from the very manner his father had spoken and from the air of watchfulness and veiled expectancy hovering about the men he had met in the last week. Nor had the Streeters been idle. Three times recently he had met strangers along the Roan Horse road, characters he recognized on sight; and later in trailing those men he had found their hoofprints going directly into Secret River. The outlaws were growing bolder and calling to their help, outside gun fighters. The underground telegraph was full of messages this early week of spring, warning even those not connected with either side. It was only the fool who saw his paradise to be the same happy, untroubled land.

"Meanwhile," muttered young Jim, "what am I going to do? I've got one gun, one head and one heart. No straddling of the fence. By the Lord, I've got to make up my mind one way or the other."

Nan Streeter let herself into the hall of the house by a certain door and stood in the darkness, listening. She recognized her father's husky, hushed voice floating from the living room and the occasional laconic interjection of a stranger. They were laying plans; that much she knew from the way her father slid his words together, piling them one atop the other, but she was much too honest to eavesdrop and after a moment of hesitation she softly opened the kitchen door and closed it behind her. Boots dragged across the floor above — other strangers turning in for the night — and at the sound of them Nan's face drew tighter. They were making this old house the resort of cutthroats and man killers, inviting the wrath of the law-abiding element of the county. War would come, soon enough, sure enough.

She went to a corner by the stove where two youngsters were sleeping on a mattress, and for a long spell she watched them, wondering what kind of men they would grow to be. There were some decent impulses in the Streeter family, but it had always seemed to her that this house with its lawless traditions had bent and warped the wills of the men folk. Once, far back, the Streeters had been honest. Then, one of them had turned lawless, and since then the dead hand of his acts had weighed heavily on them all. It was as if the succeeding generations had felt the distrust of the community and had lived up to it out of defiance. Sometimes she recognized this in herself, as when she met a sheriff or a deputy in the hills. At such times she had almost to check the instinct to fling a challenge at them and run away. That was what the Streeters had done to her and, perhaps, would do to those sleeping youngsters.

She was all the mother they had, she supplied all of the gentleness and care they had known since early babyhood. Passionately she wished them to be upright and decent, to be the kind of men young Jim Bolles was. At times she wondered if it wouldn't be best to run away with them, start them off in new surroundings. But always she came to face the one insurmountable barrier. Wherever she went she knew her brother Jere would find her and bring her and his children back. After that life would be so much the harder for them all. Jere was that way.

Even as she thought of him, a back door opened with hardly a sound and Jere slid through, his sharp eyes sweeping all the room at a single glance. He was a small man with a dark, drawn face and a narrow, feminine mouth which was forever twitching back and displaying his flashing white teeth. His motions were soft, cat-like and he was eternally watching and listening for telltale sounds.

The girl, studying him with concealed fear, was struck by the notion that all the latent evil of the Streeter heart and the Streeter blood seemed to have come to a point in him. He had the intuitive instinct of a wild animal, the treachery of a feline, the whims and volatile angers of a feline. Though he was not much older than she, his transgressions and his dissipations had left their print; he lived now on his nerves.

"Where y' been?" he demanded, looking through her with his sharp, suspicious glance.

"Out in the meadow, watching the night," said she. Always, she came as near the truth as she could, for Jere had an uncanny way of reading her voice and her eyes. Tonight he seemed unsatisfied and she thought he knew her secret. She wanted to turn away, but she knew he waited for that weakness and so she stood with her back to the wall, her hands gripped together behind her, matching his inspection with her level, sober gaze.

"Huh. You better take to staying inside, kid. It's getting unhealthy to be in the open. Where's the old man?"

She motioned toward the living room and broke into a protest. "Jere, what are you making of this ranch? All the toughs and bullies in the state are coming here! Isn't it bad enough without them? You and Dad must have lost your senses — "

He stopped her with one swift jerk of his arm. He was smiling, a smile that had no humor in it. It drew the sagging lines of his face to sharp ridges and made him seem old and dry and deadly. "No more preaching," he warned her.

"Oh, I've quit trying. But there is an end to all things, Jere. If you go beyond their patience, they will hunt you down and kill you."

"The night's been a-telling you things, eh? I guess it's getting to be public knowledge. Don't I know they aim to crucify us? Well, we aim to give 'em a surprise. When I get through this'll be a wide open county. They'll be plenty Puritans dead, kid, and the rest'll be willing enough to let us alone."

He was mad. She had feared that one day the crazy, reckless lust for killing would unhinge his caution. Now it had come about.

"Meanwhile," he went on, "you take care of things. Feed the guests we got in the morning. Me and the old man are riding tonight."

"To do what, Jere?"

Again that deadly smile brought up the dry hate in him, the suppressed murderer's instinct. "To start the ball a-rolling mebbe.

Mind your own business. And listen; don't try to run out on us. Oh, I know you been honest. You're a Streeter, too. But you ain't like ary Streeter I ever knew. And I ain't trusting nobody no more." A finger went swiftly in the direction of his sleeping sons. "I think I'd kill 'em if I thought they'd be the means of giving me away. That's for you to think about, Sis."

He left the kitchen. Presently there was a clumping of feet in the hall, a soft word or two; five minutes later she heard the two ride off. Up above the strangers were laughing, and with all her steady quiet courage she felt cold to the bone. This grim house had killed all the Streeter women — it would kill her. Once more she thought of flight. When she looked at the children she abandoned the idea. Turning, she took the lamp and went upstairs, framing it in the window a moment. That was the signal to young Jim. Then she turned down the wick, locked the door and went to bed, her mind traveling wistfully back across the ridge with the solitary rider. All her hopes and her desires were with him, yet when she came to dwell upon those hopes they seemed to vanish and leave her the more miserable.

Chapter 3

Old Jim came to the breakfast table the next morning with an ill-concealed belligerence. He roared at the Chinese cook; when the foreman came in for instructions he bit his words off in the middle; and he glowered at his son throughout the meal. Young Jim returned his treatment with a grin of delight. His father was a poor sleeper of late and the growing trouble with the Streeters only added to the old man's restlessness. The schoolmistress, likewise accustomed to these moods, chattered breezily, now and then studying young Jim covertly.

"To hear your father," said she, "it would seem he had been out late last night instead of you."

Young Jim failed to rise to the bait. His grin shortened a little, but he nodded and said he guessed he'd have to get a few wild-cats for the old gents to tear apart. Old Jim snorted at this while the schoolmistress, coming back to her target, fired a fresh shot.

"If you aren't tired of the company of a woman, perhaps you'll ride along with me to school. All this talk about war and trouble — "

"I'm sure sorry," apologized young Jim, "but I promised Joe Tatum I'd ride over to his place this morning early. I'll have Springtime go along with you."

The schoolmistress said no more, but old Jim bellowed, "Ain't this generation a polite one! In my time a lady's word was always a command."

"This is going to be a family fight in a minute," grinned young Jim, pushing back from the table. "I'm making apologies all the way around. But I guess you'll have to put up with Springtime this A.M. Sorry."

"If he casts any more sheep eyes at me," promised the lady, not without a note of irritation, "I shall pull all the whiskers out of his mustache."

"Which would be Samson shorn of his strength," said the delighted Jim. He went out to saddle her horse and to hail Springtime; and he saw them both off. The schoolmistress was almost openly hostile toward the puncher, but when young Jim saw the eagerness struggling behind Springtime's frozen face, he could hardly maintain a serious countenance. All the humor left him a few moments later, however, when his father called him to the office.

"Mebbe I'm dense in ways," said the old man, chewing on a cigar, "but that girl made some pointed remarks this morning. Are you out skylarking at night?"

"I observe the multitudinous faces of nature if that's what you mean," offered young Jim.

"Hell! Get down to facts. Are you a-going to marry the schoolma'am?" He stopped short and tried a milder tone. "You see, son, I'm getting old. Men like me don't last long. I want to see you established before I cross the hill. There's lots of ways about her I don't cotton to none whatsoever, but she's smart and she ain't flighty. As for tolerance toward the ranch hands — that'll be rubbed into her and it won't — "

Young Jim put a hand on his father's shoulder. "You're barking up the wrong tree, old-timer. In the first place, she wouldn't have a slow fellow like me. What makes you think she would? In the second place — " he hesitated, growing somber — "I might as well tell you I'm due to be single a good many years. I want Nan Streeter and she's not to be had. Not by young Jim Bolles."

The elder never moved, but young Jim thought then he had never seen such a flash of fire and fury in his father's face. Still, the old man said nothing for a long, long minute; the fury passed, leaving him a little less florid, a little less erect. Quietly he went to his desk and got his stetson. When he spoke it was with a gentleness young Jim had not heard since boyhood. "The name of Streeter is poison to me, Jim, and I reckon you know it. It goes against everything I stand for, every idea I got concerning fair play. I know the breed from the ground up. I know the devil in 'em. I've seen old Anse stab a man in the back — before your time. I know things about 'em which'd make any upright man sorry to know. How you come to be mixed up with those folks I can't see. If your heart is in that girl, I ain't got a thing to say, for I know a man's reason can't go against his heart. But just remember this, Jim: every man born of woman has got certain duties. For bad or good, he's got to stand by his kind, pay his debts. It's a matter of conscience."

He stopped, looking at his son with a quick, shy glance as if ashamed of this much self-revelation. Young Jim strode forward and gripped his father by the arm. That was all. The old man walked out and presently was galloping off toward Roan Horse. Young Jim watched him until a ridge took him from sight, then with a heavy heart he, too, got in the saddle and swung eastward to keep his word with Joe Tatum. The sun curved upward on its course and the day grew hot and pungent with the scent of the laboring earth. Dust rose along the bench where a Rocking Chair man came back from the bronc buster's camp with part of the horse herd.

"I wonder," muttered young Jim, "if he thought I wasn't thinking of my debts!"

Springtime Povy's face seldom matched his feelings. Habitually it was sad and sorrowful as if the weight of a wicked world rode on his shoulders. This morning, however, there was an internal disharmony which well accorded with that expression. Springtime had gone along with the schoolma'am bathed in a well-concealed bliss. The very proximity of the lady performed such miracles as ten bottles of Frazer's Elixir of the Seasons could not have accomplished and he only hoped that she would turn to him with a receptive countenance so that he might drop a few subtle remarks concerning the inevitable fitness of matrimony. This was Springtime's secret. The lugubrious cowpuncher, seeing himself as he wished others to see him and entirely disregarding the sorry scheme of things mortal, aspired to be educated. Not an ordinary education at the hands of an ordinary teacher in an ordinary way. He had developed, to make it plain, that fever from which there are few recoveries. The vernal urge was upon him, and he struggled dismally to find the suitable words to express it.

But he had been spared the trouble. Evelyn Fleming had penetrated that secret and this morning she had ruthlessly exposed it. In fact she had hauled it out, broke it in twain and then shattered it in such fine fragments that when the wrecking process was over, Springtime could not find so much as a forlorn splinter of his grand passion to nourish to his bosom. It may have been that the schoolma'am wanted to leave no sadly pining cowhands in her path or it may have been that her own disappointment had made her a little cruel. She gave a jab here and a thrust there, all apparently innocent and unrelated, but which left Springtime at the schoolhouse door a different man from the one who had started from the Rocking Chair gates an hour earlier.

His wooden face alone saved him. Battered and bruised, he sought the solace of the bench, making tremendous inroads on the chewing tobacco and hardly fit for the rest of the day's work. Deep and smoldering resentment was his, from which emerged one pride-salvaging thought.

"I ought to've seen she was set to have young Jim. Shucks, where's my usual good judgment? But no, I'm like all other foolish critters when it comes to connubial affection. Blind. Plumb blind. Well, if she thinks to trap Jim, she'll have her own feelin's tromped on something fierce. Yeah, won't that be too bad."

It made the dismal day seem brighter. For Springtime knew something about Jim and Nan. Not for nothing had he spent his life on the range.

"So I look like the funny man's idea of a cowboy, huh? Well, that's what she as much as said. Gosh, the more I consider it the more it stings! It sure takes a woman to stick a man with pins which don't hurt until after they're plumb sunk to the heads. All right, lady, if that's your story you hang to it. But I'll bet ten thousand steers against a buffalo chip you won't feel so pretty when young Jim waves you farewell."

If Springtime had been anything but a gentleman at heart, he would have engaged in some tall cursing. But he couldn't swear without in some manner relating the adjectives to the schoolma'am, and that obviously wouldn't do. Dark and gloomy, he walked his horse along the bench, essaying to stretch his philosophy to cover the cataclysm. If he had been a younger man, he would have rolled his blankets and left the country. Being what he was, a gentle-hearted citizen with a supreme attachment to his county and to his ranch, he dismissed the thought at once as almost disloyal and took a fresh chew.

It was at this point, while applying oil to his wounds, that he heard the echo of a shot coming off the Roan Horse road over the ridge. Right there and then his own personal troubles sank to the bottom of his head, becoming so much tinsel and gilt in a world of realities. His hand dropped halfway to his gun and he swept the country with a swift, embracing glance. A second shot followed quickly. After that silence intervened. Springtime did some quick thinking. None of the Rocking Chair men were over there. Their chores carried them back on the east range. Young Jim had gone toward Tatum's place and old Jim —

"By the hat that Maggie wears!" swore Springtime and sank his spurs into the pony's hide. They raced up along the slope with Springtime reaching down to get the rifle out of his gunboot. Fifteen minutes brought him to the crest of the ridge where he surveyed the course of the road for a half mile. What first caught his eye was the weaving figure of a horseman on the side of the ridge that shielded Secret River; the man was traveling off as rapidly as his pony would carry him. Then Springtime switched his glance lower and saw a mount he knew only too well standing in the road with the reins still hanging over its neck. Somebody lay in the road near the horse, motionless.

Springtime brought up his rifle and took one chance shot at the fugitive rider, seeing the dust kick up across the little valley. It fell far short of the man, and Springtime wasted no more time but spurred recklessly down the angle to the road. He was out of his saddle and on the dead run within ten yards of the figure. What he saw made his loyal heart swell and shrivel.

Old Jim Bolles lay there, his stetson rolled away and his white head half covered with the powdered clay of the road. He was face downward, one arm forward as if to break his fall, the other still tightly gripping the butt of his gun. A tiny rivulet of blood coursed away from his chest; when Springtime bent and put a hand to his boss's heart, it told him too plainly that the bullet had gone home. Suddenly Springtime sprang up, raging. He had caught sight of a second bullet hole entering old Jim's neck. The murderer had delivered a *coup de grâce.* More than that he had left a piece of paper in Old Jim's hand. Springtime took it and smoothed it out, reading the ill-scrawled words:

> Warning, Rockin Chare and all others. If you want to start a fight heres a chance. Leave us alone or we'l strip this valey down to rattlesnakes.

Springtime carefully folded the note and put it in his pocket, for a moment studying the vanishing figure. Pursuit wouldn't be good sense; the man could ambush him too easy, or else reach his hiding place. Anyhow, Springtime knew well enough where that figure was going. It was a matter for action a little later. Meanwhile —

He got old Jim into the saddle and climbed up behind. Whistling to the second horse he started homeward with his burden. As for the schoolma'am, she might as well never have existed for all the thought Springtime gave her. He was sounding the war drums to himself; sedate, homely dependable Springtime Povy was ready to kill.

Young Jim was still away when Springtime came home with the dead man, for which fact Springtime was mutely thankful. Being intensely shy at heart, like all men of the range, where it came to matters of the soul he didn't want to see young Jim's face when the latter looked at his father. He laid the old man on a bed in the big house, went outside and rolled himself a cigarette after cigarette, none of which he troubled to light. And when the younger Jim came riding back around noon he had fashioned the few blunt words necessary to tell the tale. Springtime was wise and he knew from experience that any injury hurt less when it was sharp and sudden; he stood up, looked once at young Jim and turned away his head, squinting at the sun.

"Your dad," said he, "is dead. I found him on the road, six miles from the school house. Potted by a gent who rode off towards Secret River. Here's the letter he left."

Jamming the piece of paper into young Jim's hand, Springtime walked off as fast as his bowed legs would allow, scarcely seeing where he went. Not for several moments did he look around, to find the door of the big house, ordinarily never shut, closed. Springtime sat on the bunkhouse steps and waited.

The dinner hour came, but no cook's triangle sounded. One by one the hands came riding in, and when Springtime told his story, they silently disappeared inside, to come out again with their cartridge belts supplied. They got their best horses from the corral, inspected their gear, looked toward the west where lay Secret River, and waited. Silently, impassively they waited for an hour or better, and when at last the door of the big house opened again and young Jim walked across the yard not a soul of them moved.

Young Jim's face was as bleak and as gray as a piece of granite stone. He swept the group as if they were entire strangers. His hand stretched forward and his finger fell from man to man.

"Smokey, you start for Roan Horse. I want the sheriff and the coroner. Jim, circle around by the Thunderbolt and tell Streibig to drop over. Just him, none of his crew. Silver, you ride to the Flying M and say the same to Mike Mitchell. Maxy, same to the Diamond Two Bar. Little Bob, to the Circle Dot. Steve, you hit for Tatum's. And Bill Jones to Bell A. That's all the riding."

As he named them they sprang to saddle and were away, riding low and fast. The sun glinted now and then on pieces of metal gear and presently there was nothing but a haze of dust to mark where they had dipped out of sight. Young Jim turned to the rest. "Limpy, you make the box. Springtime, I want you with me. Now, you boys had better get your chuck. Get on with the work around the home ranch."

Springtime tarried as young Jim walked back to the house. When his boss was out of hearing he turned on the rest of the crew and raked them with a flaming eye, almost hissing his words through his mustache. "They make men out here. Ain't I told you so!"

He knew without being told what young Jim wished of him and went toward the tool shed and got a spade and a pick. That afternoon he and young Jim dug a new grave up on the hill where the rest of the Rocking Chair dead rested. On the very summit of the plot there were two tall poplars. Under one old Jim's wife had been laid years before; under the other they meant to put old Jim.

The underground telegraph was alive that afternoon with a new message. One of the great barons had been killed; war had been declared. From ranch to ranch the news passed, was picked up and carried on from the point the Rocking Chair messenger left it. It was the eve of spring roundup, yet work stopped for the moment and men took to their horses and started north toward the Rocking Chair and the rendezvous. The warlike came because they had long been lusting for this very fight. The peaceful came because they knew the time for peace had passed. Not an old-timer within riding distance failed to ride that long afternoon, for old Jim was of their fraternity; he had fought them and he had fought with them in the ancient days. He was a part of the lifeblood and the sinew of the range, and as these old ones collected their memories came with them. There were small ranchers in the gathering, too, for they saw the challenge as all sober men saw it: the conflict of the lawless with the law they had so painfully erected. If the law fell, they fell.

By dusk it was a good-sized gathering in the Rocking Chair yard and when at midnight the sheriff and the coroner arrived, along with a preacher, it had grown to a full company of resolute, grim-faced men who waited the bidding of young Jim Bolles. The fact that the sheriff was the constituted leader of the county made no difference. This was young Jim's fight and his was the authority. A great fire had been built in front of the big house and two long tables arrayed with tin cups and plates. That fire blazed high into the opaque night, a beacon to be seen for miles and a challenge to any outpost on the ridge above Secret River. Young Jim ordered the fire for that very purpose.

With the arrival of the coroner and the preacher, the body of old Jim was carried up on the hill and put in the ground. It was a silent, tight-lipped funeral, without a woman, without tears. Springtime, standing beside the younger Jim, recalled the blunt, bearlike character of his old boss and he knew in his heart that this was the kind of ending he would have liked best: the rough good-by to one who had lived an open-handed, combative life. He caught a glimpse of young Jim's face as they turned downhill and his loyal soul rejoiced at what he saw. The flint and iron of the Bolles breed wasn't being buried that night. Springtime made for the coffee pot, noting that the sheriff and the ranch owners were going inside the big house for a powwow.

Young Jim gathered them in the office. They made a dozen all told and as he looked from man to man he felt a sudden pride in the name he carried and a quick gratefulness at the way they had responded. They had come at the call of trouble because he had asked them, fulfilling the first rule of the land. He waited until they had all crowded inside, then took the note found on his father's body and passed it to the sheriff.

"Do you recognize that writing?" he asked.

The sheriff bent over the lamp and seemed

to spell out each word. "Yep," said he. "I've seen it on bonds to keep the peace."

Young Jim took the paper and after a moment's search passed it to Tatum, his nearest neighbor. "Do you recognize it?"

Tatum went through the same motions, though faster "I reckon I do, Jim. I've had two-three letters in the same writing." He passed it back and young Jim gave it to a third man, with the same question.

"It's the identical writing of a fellow whose name I've seen on a good number of bills of lading," said the third.

"Pass it around," asked Jim. "I want everybody to have a look at it." He waited until the paper came back to him, then put a question to all of them.

"Is that the handwriting of Jere Streeter?"

Five or six of them nodded. They were certain of it. The rest had never seen Streeter's handwriting and said so.

"Well, that makes it plain enough, don't it?" put in the sheriff. "But what stings me is that he should be so blamed open and horsy about it. You'd think he was issuing a general invitation for us to come over."

"That's how it sounds," agreed Tatum. "And mebbe that's his intentions."

"Why, the crazy Piute!" grunted Streibig of Thunderbolt. "He ain't got good sense, even for a rustler. Three-four men could clean his shebang. I took Jere to have more discretion."

"Now hold on," interrupted the sheriff. "Mebbe you ain't aware he's been gathering bad men from all points of the compass. I know personal of three other Streeters who drifted in during the last week. Also I've seen about four hombres pass through Roan Horse in the same period which I wouldn't trust a busted spur with. What does that mean if not that the Streeters aim to make this their private stamping ground?"

"I've traced three trails over the ridge," added young Jim, seeming more gaunt than ever in the yellow light. Now and then the rays fell squarely on his eyes and flashed, as on the facet of a diamond.

It remained for a quiet unobtrusive man from across the Secret River to settle this point. "I guess I can settle that. This morning I had my spy glass on their yard and I counted eighteen men and two boys."

"Say twenty active guns, then," put in the impetuous Streibig. "All right. Turn this crowd loose and they'll be took before sunrise."

Young Jim shook his head. "Not that way, Streibig. I know what you're driving at. Maybe we'll have to shoot the place to pieces, but it's got to be a peaceful attempt first. Fair play, even for Streeters. There's one or two who'd like to come out of that hole without bloodshed."

Most of them knew whom he meant and they looked away from him, uncomfortable. "We want Jere for murder," he went on. "We think we want him and his dad, and the two hands he keeps most of the time, for rustling. But how about proof?"

"Here," said Streibig, pulling something from his pocket. "I been waiting for your dad to start the ball rolling or I'd acted myself. Here's proof." He shoved an irregularly oblong piece of cowhide into the light. "This mark, as me and my men can testify, was blotched. We caught the critter down in the brakes of the Secret River, running in the Streeter home herd. It bore one of their three brands, the Lazy L Diamond T. But we shaved the hair off and found the ridges where our own iron had burnt our Thunderbolt on it. See what he did?" To make it clear to all he took his pencil and marked his own Thunderbolt brand on a piece of paper. To illustrate the way the Streeters had changed it he drew three short intersecting lines and produced the Lazy L Diamond T. "There's the proof. Look at it."

All looked at it, though none of them needed much of a glance to see what had been done. The rumor of this had already gone abroad and most of them knew, without being able to prove which brands the Streeters were tampering. Streibig went on. "Why, Jim, your own brand has been switched, too. It ain't no job to take a Rocking Chair and make a Circle H of it."

Young Jim nodded. "I know it. Dad had an inspector down at the stock yards in Portland watching for that. Said the inspector was sending him proof. It hasn't got here yet."

"Well," said Streibig, "that blotched Thunderbolt is enough to convict 'em, if it's proof you want. As for me, I want that nest of thieves and killers just naturally wiped out."

So did the rest of them, including the sheriff who was heartily tired of being blamed for not bringing them in. They said as much or looked as much.

Young Jim straightened, eyes traveling from one to the other. "I know. I guess I've got more of a personal interest than the rest of you boys. But it's on both sides. There's my cards on the table. Plain slaughter won't help me, boys. You can't bring a man to life by shooting ten others. I want the Streeters alive if we can get 'em. Let the law hang Jere, which it will. But if they won't come alive, then we'll get them, dead!" The last word fell flatly in the room. Young Jim's eyes flashed again in the light and the lines of his face stretched like cords and vanished. The light faded. "All but one, boys. I want her alive. There's one good Streeter in that crowd."

Silence again. The sheriff put out his arm and let it fall lightly across young Jim's shoulder. "All right, boy. This is sure tough on you. It sure is. Name your men."

"My crew and myself make sixteen. You fellows will bring the posse to twenty-eight. That's plenty."

"Let's go, then," said the sheriff.

One by one they filed out. As they came from the house the waiting crowd outside stirred and moved toward them. Young Jim, knowing all that power stood behind him, should have been glad. Instead he had the appearance of a man seeing ghosts. He drew a sharp breath and spoke to them.

"I'm obliged, boys, but the posse's picked. Help yourself to the chuck and sleep on the place. Everything on this ranch is open to you, now and as long as I'm alive. If any of you ever get in trouble, all you've got to do is ask me for help. As long as I've got a dollar in the bank or a cow on the range, it's yours."

There was a murmur that seemed to be of discontent. Young Jim quelled it by spreading out his arms. The firelight fell fully on his body, on his face. "Stand behind us and let us do it in our own way."

After that there was no trouble. The men of the posse ate quickly, without relish, and gathered to one side. Young Jim rode to the front and said, "Let's go." The twenty-eight of them went down the road, crossed the creek and turned up the ridge, over which lay Secret River and the Streeter ranch.

From her bedroom window the schoolmistress saw them file out of the light into the darkness. She had witnessed old Jim's body go up the hill to be buried; she had seen that blood-red fire leaping toward the sky and the faces of the hundred men illuminated by it — faces in which she seemed to see mirrored the lust and the barbaric cruelty of this grim land. She had heard young Jim quell them with his quiet words; she had seen them eat and drink on the eve of death, noted the glint of their eyes and the hard bulge of their jowl muscles.

It had all been a night of horror to her. Through the veil of prosaic life, through the daily humdrum of routine, of jest and of petty incident had come this smashing, crimson, primitive force. Out of it all stood one great figure — that of young Jim who with his grief locked within him still had a place for a little charity in his heart. So she watched him go. And while the terror of the scene clutched her, she wished she was enough of his kind of woman to ride with him.

Chapter 4

Once again young Jim traveled the trail he knew so well, and once again the unfathomed immensity of the sky, the sweet smell of the sage, and the solace and the mystery of the deep night were wrapping around him and tugging at his spirit. But the old charms went unheeded, the old images failed to rise in his mind. Instead, he kept seeing his father's massive face as it had been in their last talk and he heard his father's voice, saying over and over again, "A man's got his duties to do, his debts to pay. It's a matter of conscience." Well, he was paying his debts now, paying them down to the last red cent, even though it left him impoverished in happiness. What was happiness, after all, but an illusive shadow which men ruined themselves in seeking? Hadn't everything in this vague world, from the highest start to the smallest form of life in the earth, told him time and time again that destiny marched on regardless of things living or dead? He was but an instrument moved by the supreme force that moved them all.

Had he been a small man, young Jim would have turned everlastingly bitter in the course of the night. Instead, the straightforward simpleness and the sweetness of his nature kept him steady. He had made up his mind to go through with his chore, whatever it cost, while at the same time he meant to do whatever he could to bring Nan Streeter out of the sinister circle of men holding her.

They crawled up the side of the ridge, silent save for the slapping of stirrup leather and the subdued squeaking of gear. Springtime rode immediately behind him and the rest came along at close intervals until they had reached the crest and were halfway down the other side. Here young Jim stopped. Below, in the midst of that black depression, stood the Streeter ranch where usually a light glimmered. Tonight no light winked upward at him; they were all asleep or they were all waiting for the posse's approach. A horse crunched on its bit and someone whispered.

The sheriff pushed alongside, murmuring, "That fence is going to make it mean. I've studied considerable, but I dunno whether it's best to dismount and crawl through or open the gate farther down."

"Better crawl through," said young Jim. They advanced with redoubled caution; a single rock started down the incline would be plain warning to the outlaws, a possible instrument of ambush. Young Jim, seeing the dips and curves of the hillside as though it were in plain daylight, left the trail and quartered to avoid a bow of the river. Presently his senses told him they were at the fence. He dismounted and laid his hand across the top strand of wire, hearing the sheriff grope beside him.

"Better pass the word back to spread out and crawl through," whispered young Jim. "Easy does it. Best to tell off the flank men by name so they'll understand they're to go all around the place. We want it girdled. No firing unless warning's given or the Streeters start it. Better have a countersign, too, or we'll be shooting each other. Make it 'Rocking Chair' and 'Thunderbolt.' "

This trickled back, a piece at a time. There was a subdued rustling of sage, a soft dragging of spurs. Young Jim spoke again. "Sheriff, Springtime, Joe Tatum — you boys come with me."

He eased himself through the wire and waited a moment until the others had joined him. Ten yards ahead he brought up against a shed. Touching the men beside him, he stopped, listening.

Secret River rippled against the willows fifty yards away; a small wind splashed through the top of a pine. Other than that there was nothing to guide them. Directly in front, making a dim bulk against the shadows, stood the main house, seeming tenantless. Young Jim put his ear against the shed's side and rested thus for five minutes — or until the sheriff began to be impatient. Touching his partners as a signal, he skirted the shed, reached a little path and came to the edge of the house porch.

It had been a matter of ten minutes, more or less, since the three of them had passed the barbed wire, time enough for the converging flanks of the party to have traversed their respective arcs of the circle. Young Jim studied the ink-black corners of the porch with a hard, quick glance before announcing himself. "Down you fellows. Flat." He waited until he heard them drop. Springtime's protesting mutter floated upward. "Don't be a galoot now, Jim. This ain't no basket social." Young Jim's fingers brushed the butt of his gun; he straightened, stepped on the porch and walked across it, thrumming the door with his knuckles. His voice carried out over the meadow, audible to everybody.

"Open up, inside. This is young Jim Bolles. I want to see Jere Streeter!"

It seemed that the weight of the world converged upon that little porch. In the silence the rustling waters of the river grew noisier to men's ears and every minute sound along the meadow had the effect of a rifle shot. Young Jim waited, hearing Springtime's teeth click on his tobacco cud. The sheriff sighed and rolled along the ground, whispering. "You'll get no answer out of that house tonight, boy."

He was wrong. Something groaned inside. A body moved, a woman's voice called through the door. "Jim — go back! Oh, go away before you are killed."

Young Jim leaned against the wall. "Open up, Nan. I've got to see Jere."

"Jere is not in the house. There's no one here but the boys and me. Jim, you are walking straight to death."

Silence. She had never lied to him, yet he understood well enough she would lie to shield him, to prevent the spilling of blood.

"Tell Jere to come out peaceably. I want him. If there's others inside, tell them to put aside their guns. We've got the house blocked. Nobody wants a war, nobody wants a lynching. But we've come to take Jere, your dad and the two hired hands. The others are free to go."

She struck the door with her hand as if to make him believe her. "But there's no one in here you want, Jere. Believe me!"

"Then open the door," said young Jim in a half audible voice. "Light a lamp and put it in the hall."

"That's — that's murder!" The words hardly passed through the wooden barrier. Young Jim shook his head.

"Open it, Nan. Light the lamp."

He heard her going back. A hinge squealed, something fell to the floor. Springtime growled, "Step aside when that thing opens, Jim. You'll make a good target." Yellow light slid through the edges of a kitchen blind and the hinge protested again. She was at the door, speaking as she turned the key. "Be careful, Jim." Then the portal swung back and she stood before him, holding the lamp behind her to keep the rays from revealing him too fully. He had a word in his mouth, yet it died there. He had never seen her so tall, so straight. Tragedy had made her stately; it had made her beautiful. When she spoke her voice echoed richly down the hall. "I give you my word, Jim. I'm alone in here with the boys. But tell your men outside to take care of themselves."

He slipped through, with Springtime and the sheriff dodging in behind him. Presently Joe Tatum and Streibig and three or four others followed, closing the door behind them. Young Jim took the lamp from her. She gave the others one quick glance and turned back to him.

"I knew you would come with them," she said. "You couldn't help it."

He nodded, slowly. "You know why we are here?"

"You want my folks for what they have done."

The rest of the men were creeping through the house. Young Jim saw that she didn't know and he thought for a moment that it was best not to tell her. But when he realized how steadfast she was in staying on and sharing the Streeter fortunes he understood that it needed a shock to weaken her resolution.

"It's murder, Nan. Jere killed my father at noon today on the Roan Horse road."

Of a sudden the house was full of protesting noises and the men were calling from various rooms. Another light flared out of an inner door and Springtime's voice rose in a kind of singsong profanity. "If this ain't enough to send a man to drink! By gollus, I'm sweating like — "

"Jim, I'd rather have had him kill me. If someone had only shot that first evil Streeter — "

"It's over now," he broke in roughly. "No man knows how the cards will fall. But this house has seen the last of you. Get the kids. I'll have somebody ride back to the Rocking Chair with you."

He saw her head move from side to side. "It's too late. Why do you want to protect me?"

"You know the answer to that. I'm not changing. Come."

"What kind of woman would I be to marry you now?" she demanded with a show of spirit. "If I did, the valley ought to tar and feather me. Jim, it's not stubbornness that keeps me here now. But — I've got to see it out. Down to the very end. There's nothing else to do."

"You don't owe the Streeters anything," said he, growing conscious of the passing time. "Will you tell me where they went?"

He saw her head move again and of a sudden he knew that he had to smash the spell that held her. It was neither loyalty to her clan, nor pride; it was only that she would involve no one else in the tangle of her life. She, too, paid her debts. Young Jim raised his arm. "I give you three minutes to get your things. If you won't go of your own accord, then I'm taking you."

Of a sudden her will seemed to give away. "Oh, then — wait until I find the boys." She vanished into the darkness of the kitchen as the sheriff came down the stairs. "They've scooted," he grumbled. "Worse and more than that. There's a rheumatic feeling in my bones, Jim, which is sure a sign of trouble. It's too blamed quiet. They ain't far off, I'll bet a hen. Guess we'll just have to stay put till daylight."

Young Jim heard the children running toward the corner of the house. The girl seemed to be whispering, directing them. Cold air struck him in the face and there was the slamming of a door. The sheriff whirled around, gun half out as young Jim raced to the end of the hall, then into the kitchen. No one there. He tried the back door — and found it locked. The sheriff ran to the opposite end of the hall, swearing. "If this ain't the damnedest mess I was ever in! Say, this door's locked, too. How in hell did she vamoose?"

Springtime popped out of the living room; Streibig and Tatum walked down the stairs, followed by the others. "She's an empty house," announced Tatum. "I guess they lost their nerve."

The long silence of the meadow was broken by the sharp crack of a gun and a man's high yell. On the instant the whole clearing flamed with gunplay. The sheriff swung about and galloped to the door. "Come on," he cried. "For all we know they mebbe have this joint mined with dynamite! By Godfrey, if this ain't — "

The words trailed off to nothing. He had opened the front door and started through. A board two feet away from young Jim showed a splintered furrow; the sheriff coughed once and bowed his head, falling across the threshold. Young Jim saw a hole in the man's head and the quick jet of blood that spurted from it. Raising the lamp high he smashed it against he wall and in the subsequent darkness jumped out of the place, Springtime running abreast of him, Tatum and Streibig at his heels.

Nan Streeter had vanished in thin air; the sheriff was down; war had started in deadly earnest.

"Two dead men I've seen this day!" wheezed Springtime. "Don't nobody be fooled. This is a-going to be one hell-bent scrape! Which way, Jim?"

"Down flat!"

The party dropped to the ground all in a heap. "Us charging across the meadow like that might stampede the crowd or draw fire," said young Jim. A bullet struck the house directly behind him and he raised his voice. "None of the Streeters in this circle, boys. Turn those slugs the other way. Easy on the shells. We've got plenty of time!"

His words carried on up the slope of the ridge and a booming, ribald challenge came back. "You sure have got plenty of time, amigo! Plenty time to die! We got you dished right where we want you, see? Try and get out!"

"Which statement," said Springtime, "contains the kernel of truth. Now where in hell did that big bazoo come from?"

"I think they're bunched on the ridge," replied Streibig. "Say, we must've come right close to 'em when we rode down the slope. Now ain't they sly? It ain't a bad start; no, sir."

"Watch for gun flashes," grunted Joe Tatum. "That fellow was talking for advertising purposes. They got a joker up their elbows."

"Now I know how Custer felt," said Springtime cheerfully. "Say, this ground is awful doggoned damp."

Young Jim's eyes roved through space, catching here and there the purplish red flame of a rifle shot. The firing had dropped to an intermittent sputtering; it seemed to him that the renegades had taken a fixed position along the opposite side of the fence and about twenty feet up the slope. They were not a hundred yards off and spread in an irregular line. How long that line was he couldn't determine, but he had the suspicion that there were some of them considerably out on the flank, reserving their fire in case of an attempt on the part of the posse to skirt them. It was a clever arrangement and it bore the print of Jere Streeter's quick, treacherous mind. He said as much to his partners and heard Joe Tatum's fist thump the ground in anger. "By gum, he'd better be clever. It's his neck we're a-going to get."

Springtime had turned himself end for end, making a discovery. "Say, they got three-four men over across the river in case we should swim thataway!"

Young Jim likewise swung and presently saw a gun flash up along the rocks. Another angle covered. Jere Streeter had let the posse go unopposed down into the clearing and had posted his men so as to form a more or less effective net around them. The river and a handful of renegades hemmed the posse on the west; while on their east the main body of the Streeters made a semi-circle, both ends of which touched the river. Apparently it was like this; no gun flashes issued from along the river bank, but young Jim, trying to read the whole of Jere Streeter's plan, gave him credit for overlooking no bets. Evidently the renegades meant to wait until daybreak and pick off the posse at leisure.

"We got in here and we can get out," he said to himself. Jere Streeter, uncanny at understanding men's motives, had seemed to bank on the fact that young Jim would want to settle the fight peacefully and would therefore walk up on the house and ask for a parley. "I give him credit," he added. "But what's been done can be undone. We've got a man for each of his men, and a few to spare." He made his arrangements on the spot and offered them to the little group. "If they fooled us, we can fool them. I'm betting their flanks extend pretty well to the river. But we'll have to find a way through. What we'll do is take about ten men each, in two parties. Streibig, you take one party and go north along the river bank. Tatum, you take the other and go south. It'll be right down on your bellies all the way until you're certain you've got some hundred yards behind them. Then crawl up on the bench and circle back so you've got them topped. But don't fire. Settle right down and wait for daylight. When they start firing on us down here, you boys open up from behind. They'll be between fires. I'll send three-four fellows across the stream to take care of those over there. The rest of us'll stick here."

"Sounds like turkey to me," observed the active Tatum. Streibig agreed it was a sound move and got on his knees.

"Take every other man from the circle until you've got your number," said young Jim. "When you get started, I'll have the boys do a lot of useless firing to make noise. It'll cover you a little."

The two of them went off without further parley. Springtime rolled over again and groaned. "I wish I had a cigarette. Jim, did it ever occur to you they's something dag-goned funny about this rancho which ain't had any satisfactory explaining? How did that gal vamoose in the house? Why is it nobody ever tracked a Streeter all the way home?"

Young Jim's arm reached out and fell on Springtime's shoulder. "That's been on my mind the last half hour, Springtime. I've got a hunch which we'll proceed to use in a minute. Nan Streeter's inside our lines. I'm betting all I got on it and I mean to find her before daylight. Right now you start to the left and tell the boys to fire up for about five or ten minutes. I'll take the right."

Young Jim crawled straight forward until he reached the nearest man. When he got within speaking distance he heard the fellow grunt and the snapping of a gunbolt. "Easy," said Young Jim.

It was one of his own men, Little Bob. The man swore sulphurically. "I'd rather go down in a skunk's burrow, I'd rather. Christopher! All I hone for is a sight of something solid."

"That's coming," said young Jim. He followed the line until he collided with Springtime. The two of them crawled riverward, passed the word to the adjoining men of the posse, and crept beyond the circumference of the circle. Water gurgled in their ears. Springtime's voice broke between a whisper and a cough. "Swimming the river, Jim?"

"No. Stick close. We're going down to water's edge and travel right along the willows. Hold your breath."

They dropped down a straight three feet, threaded the willows and dropped another short distance until the wet sand bubbled around their boots. Springtime turned his bootheel against a stone and suppressed a groan. A rifle spat from across the stream, the willows weaved in the wind, and the whole meadow rang with the suddenly concerted fusillade of the posse. Young Jim slid between the bushes, exploring the sandy bluff. Twenty yards along he stopped dead, his ears turned against the breeze; and as suddenly he swung away until he stood almost knee-deep in the water.

Something stirred along that shelving; stirred and stopped; a twig snapped, audible even above the intermittent noise of the firing. The outlaws across the stream, stirred by the posse's activity, began pumping slugs into the meadow; a bullet fell into the water with a sharp *plunk,* and in a moment a second struck the sand bluff. Still young Jim held his place. Whoever was over on the narrow strip of beach seemed likewise waiting. Springtime's arm crawled slowly downward; the firing in the meadow dwindled — and the willows moved again under a body. Young Jim stepped up on the sand, crouched low and murmured, "Thunderbolt."

Springtime dived past him, water spraying high; flame streaked out in the heavy darkness and a man said, "Come on, you yellowbelly!" Young Jim, rising, was met with the full impact of another. He brought up his gun, swinging it sidewise for the man's head, not daring to shoot because of Springtime's position. The barrel grazed his opponent's head and was wrenched from his hand by the downward force of its arc. Together they went over into the water, young Jim's face going below the surface. He raised his knees into the bulk atop him, drawing a guttural cry of rage for his effort. Then he was over and up and had hold of a gun. Powder belched in his face and his ears seemed to crack and lose their power. His free fist struck soft flesh and his lurching shoulder caught the man flush under the jaw; the gun was his. This time it struck home and all resistance ebbed. Rising up, he heard Springtime swearing broadly. "Some son-of-a jackass took me a-plenty! I got one hombre! The other went a-galloping off!"

Young Jim heard the threshing of the fugitive in the willows. Stumbling on, he was slapped soundly in the eyes by their weaving branches and when he pulled them clear, the noise of the fleeing one no longer echoed on the beach. Springtime had lost his path and was ten feet behind; and as young Jim cleared the willows a full current of cold air beat against his face, steadier and chillier than that of the night breeze. He took another pace forward and was away from it. Turning on his heels, he climbed the sand bank, threaded another of the willow clumps and quite suddenly found himself with his head scraping the roof of a passageway leading directly back under the meadows. One stray echo came rolling out toward him.

"Springtime," he murmured, "you stick right here. I'm investigating this."

He thought the puncher heard him above the vagrant echoes and the swishing of the brush. Reaching out, he felt the sides of the tunnel lead away and he stepped into it and followed its windings.

Within ten feet young Jim was on his knees, the sides of the tunnel cramping around him; it continued to narrow as he proceeded until he was flat on his stomach, hitching ahead a foot at a time. He shoved the captured gun in his holster, fearing to jam the muzzle with the crumbling earth; it was a weird, unsafe place for a man to be traversing, the dampness condensing to a kind of slime along the bottom. He knew, too, that others had preceded him, for he felt the print of their boot toes still in the mud and the furrows on each side where their elbows had gouged.

But he was not prepared for what followed. Inching ahead, he felt a quivering of the ground above and there came to him a faint reverberation of the posse's gunfire. The breeze in the tunnel seemed to swell and his exploring fingers discovered a sudden lifting and widening of the passageway. He raised himself and stepped ahead, lost his balance on what seemed to be a kind of chute and tumbled over, falling almost the length of his body and landing on a wood floor. A blunt instrument pressed against his back and a sibilant whisper warned him.

"Damn you, you're dead if you move. All right, Bill, get a rope. No, wait, this is easier."

Young Jim realized of a sudden he had reached a vault directly underneath the Streeter house; the boards above him protested with the weight of softly moving bodies. Jere Streeter had played his joker.

A gun barrel came crashing down on Jim's head and he fell senseless.

Chapter 5

Young Jim woke in some remote and stuffy room to the sound of a muffled crying. It penetrated the fog of his brain and the violent throbbing of his head and it served to bring the strength back to him; for it was a woman crying, and he knew only one woman to be with the Streeters. At the same time he was reminded of an ache in his arms, together with the prickling sensation of sleep along his fingers. He waggled them, discovering that he had been tightly bound, the cord pressing deeper into his flesh as he made an effort to release it. That same rope circled his legs.

But it was not so much his own plight that worried him. He had been in tighter places before without losing his head. It was Nan's suppressed breathing coming from somewhere out of the dark. That coupled with the knowledge that here in this ramshackle house a part of the renegades waited for dawn to pour their fire into the backs of his own men. This was Jere Streeter's joker. The treacherous, clever one had slipped along the river bank with a few of his followers and gone through the tunnel; or else he had been down in the vault beneath the house when the posse entered and searched it. Young Jim had no certain knowledge, either, that Jere was with this party of the outlaws, but the more he thought of the situation the more he was sure this would be the very spot the man would choose. For Jere would undoubtedly place himself where the greatest killing would be. Daylight must surely be just below the horizon; the posse had left the Rocking Chair at midnight and that was all of three hours ago. Or better.

Young Jim turned his head to find a hint of the graying shadows and saw nothing but gloom. He rolled over, to strike a wall. Reversing his direction he hit another wall. Then he slid toward his feet, to touch a third barrier. The sound he made seemed all out of proportion to the force of his blow and he knew then they had chucked him in a closet. A closet in a room upstairs, for he could hear the swish of the wind on the eaves above his head.

The crying had stopped, the rifle fire had

stopped, nor could he make out any other noise inside the place. It were as if both parties bided their time and saved their ammunition for the bitter encounter sure to follow upon the first crack of light. The thought made young Jim desperate; he hitched himself to a sitting position and after a few preliminary efforts got to his feet, scraping the top of the closet with his head. Presently he found the door knob and turned about to grasp it with his hands. It gave. He slid out of the closet and stood plastered to a wall, listening. The perceptibly graying light of false dawn came through the windows, and he thought he heard a murmuring below him, though he wasn't sure. In such a place the imagination created ghost people and ghost echoes. Young Jim tried to shake the steady ache from his head, fighting with the rope that held him.

Again the faint sliver of a sound. Young Jim collected his muscles, waiting, knowing somebody had entered the room. A sigh, a mutter and then a muttered phrase, "By the hat that Maggie wore — "

"Springtime!"

Springtime moved with all the stealthiness of a cat. In a moment he had reached young Jim, his breath rising and falling as if from great exertion. He put his mouth to young

Jim's ear and though both of them had their lives in pawn he could not suppress his habitual dry humor. "I bet I've died a dozen times in the last twenty minutes. Knowed you'd reco'nize my private cussword if you heard it — if you was alive."

"Which is queer," murmured young Jim.

Springtime's knife sought the rope. "Being alive? No. Jere wants private revenge on you. I heard it. Yeah. When I lost you by the river, I stumbled around till I found the tunnel. Come into the cellar. Knowed then they was some of the outlaws in the house. Streaks back and warns the fellas. Took off my boots and crawled through again. They's about six guys in this place, all posted around windows. That's how I got through the hall without them hearing me. I ketched Jere's voice a-speaking about you and I sorta gathered you was up here."

The rope fell from young Jim's body and Springtime shoved a gun into his hands. Now that he was with his boss again he forsook all initiative.

"How in hell are we a-going to get out of this?"

It had been only a matter of minutes, this meeting, yet it was growing distinctly grayer — gray enough for him to see the bulk of Springtime's body. Standing here, he reviewed the situation. Streibig and Tatum were along the ridge. Springtime's warning should have brought a couple of the posse to cover the tunnel mouth. The rest of the men were in the meadow, knowing that the house held outlaws, and probably they had found shelter against the raking fire that would soon come. All they needed was a word to set them going. Well, there was but a single thing to do now; sweep the house clean before the outlaws on the ridge got a fair sight of their target. It was light enough for close fighting; in a half hour the mists would thin out sufficiently to move against the remainder of the band.

He thought of the girl, crouched somewhere in another room and he checked a strong desire to hunt her out. He could not risk crossing the creaking floors and thus giving himself away. Bending toward Springtime he whispered, "Cover the head of the stairs. The play's about to get going."

Springtime crept back and presently young Jim saw him leaning against the banister, gun drawn. Going to a window he tested the catches; they were loose and the sashes seemed to run free. At a single motion he flung the window up, bent out and sent a shout rocketing across the meadow. "Come on Rocking Chair, clean out the house first!

There's six of 'em below! Springtime and me'll keep 'em from coming above."

He heard a high, shrill yell, the first crack of a gun; then the meadow flamed at a dozen different points and the house shook with the replying fire. Springtime was cursing in a round, singsong voice, flinging his challenge down the stairway. "Come on, you tunnel rats! Who's first up to die first?"

The men in the meadow seemed to have drawn closer to the house and posted themselves near the porch and the lower openings after Springtime had passed the word to them, for their assault marched close on the heels of young Jim's shout. He heard the crash of glass, thick passionate oaths and the trembling of the whole ancient structure as he raced to join Springtime. Men were scurrying through the hallway converging upon it and swirling together in a solid mass. Out of this jam two or three flung themselves and started up the stairs.

Young Jim cried, "Thunderbolt," and held his fire an instant. There was no answer to it, save Springtime's rough prophecy, "Here's where somebody goes to hell!" and their guns roared together. The railing to the stairway gave and the oncoming figures spilled over it, back upon the heads of those below. Flame and fury swept that gray space; somebody was crying like a child down there, and somebody spent his last breath in a vicious, unprintable farewell. The posse had made a breach. One moment the guns roared and figures were locked together; and then it was deathly still and young Jim heard men drawing deep breaths, queerly relapsing to half whispers.

Young Jim started down the stairs. "Springtime, you rummage the rooms. Nan's somewhere about. Bring her outside of this slaughter pen." He tarried long enough to strip off his coat and fling it back to the puncher. "It's dead cold out. Put this around her!" Then he was collecting the posse. "Cover the lower door, boys. Let's see what we've got. There's a lamp in the kitchen. Jere ought to be among these dead ones."

Yellow light guttered and revealed the hall, glinting on a pool of blood, on the faces of the dead and the crippled. Young Jim's eyes raced along the five men down and he shook his head in a sharp, angry manner when he saw one of his own men, Little Bob, sprawled lifeless. Old man Streeter, Nan's father, was right at the foot of the stairs, one arm lying upward on the steps. Two unknown men, part of the Streeter reinforcements, were likewise dead. Another of them sat with his back to the wall, nursing a shoulder and looking at them all with livid hate. But nowhere could he see Jere Streeter. The ringleader had fled. That much was certain as members of the posse came back from their search. Young Jim found the trap door leading down into the cellar and threw it open, passing the lamp below the floor and swiftly scanning the pit. None of the crowd had had time to go that way evidently. He dropped the trap door and stationed a man by it.

"Maybe Jere started through the tunnel. We'll find out. Now, back to the clearing. We've got some more eggs to fry."

They had crushed a part of Jere Streeter's army. The taste of blood was in their throats as they came running out of the place and faced the ridge along which the main body of outlaws waited. Morning fog swirled heavily above their heads, rising an inch at a time, shutting off one party from the other. But the fight in the house had made those on the hillside uneasy, and a sporadic and aimless volley of shots began ripping along the meadow turf. Young Jim collected his men and pointed toward the line of loose rock and rubble just beyond the fence.

"Dig in there, boys. Don't push 'em yet. They've got the long end of the teeter on us. Just spread out and get set. Streibig and

Tatum will open in a minute. That's all the notice we want."

He turned, to find Springtime coming out of the house with Nan Streeter and the two lads. And though the blood in him was hot, the sight of the girl seemed to chill him to the marrow. That clear proud face he had worshiped was marked with bruises that were deep blue; her wrists as she held them out were bleeding.

Springtime looked at his boss with the face of a wild man, exclaiming, "I'm in favor of slicing somebody an inch at a time, the black, snake-hearted buzzard."

She stumbled and young Jim sprang forward to hold her; he saw her dark eyes filled with a horror and her mouth quivering with pain. "Nan!" he muttered, huskily "Who in God's name — "

She tried to smile, but failed utterly. Her lips formed a phrase. "Jere — he's out of his head — he thinks I've betrayed him. Jim, I'm weak — oh, so weak!"

Young Jim's face turned bleak. "He got away from us, Nan. Lord help you, girl, but I'm going to kill him with my own two fists! No gun, you hear? I'll find Jim and break him with my hands!"

A sudden swelling of rifle fire warned him. He turned to Springtime. "You take care of her, old-timer. Don't leave her, understand? If we push these fellows back, you get her and the kids on horses and make tracks for Rocking Chair."

Springtime looked at him almost pleadingly, but young Jim shook his head. "It's a special favor I ask, Springtime."

"Oh, well," said the disappointed cowpuncher, "live and let live. Mebbe I can put in a bullet or two anyway."

Young Jim ran to the fence and ducked through. A bullet chipped a rock at his very feet and he dropped flat, looking up in time to see the edge of the mist rising. Like a curtain above a row of rifle barrels.

He shouted "Streibig — Tatum! Let's go!"

These two wings up on the ridge had already started; young Jim began to crawl along from boulder to boulder, hearing the *ping* of a bullet pass him. Coming to better shelter, he scooped out a little earth and looked along the rising ground. A stetson showed above a rock — an old ruse that failed to draw his fire. Presently the stetson dropped down and a gun barrel poked around the rock. Young Jim took careful aim just above that barrel and held his breath. A head sidled to view; young Jim fired and saw the barrel drop to the ground.

That shot seemed to unleash the latent

savagery of every man along the ridge. The whole valley reverberated with the crack of guns and the high yells of challenge and answering defiance. Young Jim's line of men blazed away, putting a barrage over the heads of the outlaws, at the same time working forward along the slope. They would have suffered severely for this had not Streibig's and Tatum's parties, high above all others, swept the outlaws with a sure, unerring accuracy. This caused the outlaws to swing and divide their attention.

Save for this nutcracker arrangement it would have been a long-drawn debate, an all-day sniping of opposing factions. But the outlaws, once so sure of themselves, felt the weakness of their position and young Jim began to see a shifting and a sliding off along the flanks. Tatum, on the south, likewise saw it and, being a man who chafed at all form of restraint and whose blood had long boiled at the thought of the injustice and lawlessness along Secret River, he suddenly popped up from his covert and swung his hat above him for all the world to see.

"Come on, let's make this a fight! They're a-running." His party scrambled out of the rocks to a man and began galloping downward upon the outlaws, guns flashing.

Young Jim lost no time. He, too, rose

from concealment and pressed upward. There was no need for him to urge his men; they were abreast of him in a moment, ducking, weaving, firing on the run. All that had gone on before was but child's play to this. The scum of the earth, the sweepings of the county opposed them; men who fought with a price on their heads. The fire withered the short stretch of hill and young Jim, now and then sparing a glance to right and left, saw some of his men go down; always it tightened his throat and sent raging hot words to his lips. He clawed at the great boulders in his path, reached a depression and leaped at an outlaw crouched in the bottom of it. Flame and smoke spat in his face; his arm quivered and he found himself sprawled atop a figure that neither moved nor spoke. He rested a moment on his hands and knees, the dead one frowning at him; when he got to his feet the whole scene had changed.

The posse had broken the resistance, smothering the renegades between converging walls of bullets. To his left, a dozen of Streeter's men stood together, hands in the air. From the other flank came gunfire cracks where three or four individuals went on, but these were swift-ending affairs. As he watched, he saw the posse close around them, heard an abrupt command. Young Jim stared from man to man, searched the silent figures huddled on the ground, failing to find the face he wanted to see.

"Damn the man! Why don't he stay and fight it out?"

But Jere Streeter, who seemed always to have one more trick up his sleeve, had wriggled free, leaving the crowd to its fate. The last shot cracked across the meadow; Streibig and Tatum were herding the prisoners together, none too gently, while some of the Rocking Chair men traversed the slope to find their dead. Of a sudden everyone looked worn and dispirited. The fighting edge evaporated in the chilly morning air. Shoulders drooped and words were spoken in a kind of monotone.

All but Tatum. He turned to young Jim, still afire. "We've lost five fine fellows to herd this riffraff. Somebody ought to pay for it, Jim! By Godfrey, I'm for lining out some of 'em — shooting 'em down!"

"You don't mean it, Joe," said young Jim, shaking his head. "You're just talking now to hear yourself."

"The job's done," put in Streibig, passing a hand across his bloodshot eyes. "I ain't a bit sorry, either. What'll we do with the critters?"

"Herd them along to the Rocking Chair,"

said young Jim. "We'll rest there a spell and — "

He said no more. Far to the south his glance had been arrested by the figure of a man spurring up out of a depression. Young Jim raced toward the horses, both Tatum and Streibig at his heels. He waved them back. "It's my fight! I'll finish it alone!"

He reached his horse, swung up and galloped by the gathered men. Springtime shouted something from the house and seemed on the point of leaving the girl. Young Jim waved his arm toward the Rocking Chair. "Take her there, Springtime! I'm riding alone!"

In a moment he was out of earshot. At the top of the ridge he caught another short view of the fugitive and he knew it was Jere Streeter's thin, wasted body, swaying in the saddle. He bent low and urged his horse to a steady gallop. Over the crest they went, meadow and river and all the men dropping away behind.

As he pursued Jere Streeter, he knew that but one of them would ever return; it could be no other way. Jere could not be taken alive. As for himself, he was glad of it. Young Jim had aged during that memorable night; something had happened to him. He had started from Secret River, willing to turn

Jere over to the law, willing to let the impersonal machinery of justice deal out punishment. Now he knew that the law had no meaning for him; he, who had always opposed his father's rough and ready manner of settling trouble by direct action, was about to adopt those very tactics. He recalled a remark his father had once made.

"The law is fine, Jim. It keeps a balance in this here world. But remember one thing; there's a code in the country which the law can't touch. When one fellow passes the lie, or when he deliberately lays down a challenge to a second party, that second party is a yellow dog if he tries to screen himself with the law. Oh, I know the East calls us a bunch of highbinders because of that code. But they don't live like we do. The law protects 'em at every point. Out here we've got to protect ourselves in lots of things. Courage and a reputation for never backing down is something you've absolutely got to maintain. Once the roughs and the toughs and the gun toters know you ain't got sand in your craw, they'll make life so mis'able you might as well pull out of the country and go to clerking."

He had accused his father more than once of clinging to outgrown ways. Today he recalled the elder had been wise. Here was a thing he, young Jim, had to settle with his own hands. There was nothing else to do.

Over the eastern rim the sun was breaking, lighting the land with a rose flame. A creek ran away toward Secret River all a-sparkle; the alders along it were emerald green. In the distance a scattered band of Rocking Chair stock made dun colored blotters against the earth. As he breathed the clear air, redolent of pine and sage and upshooting grasses, he knew of a sudden that all he was or ever would be came of the West and belonged to the West. He was part of it; it was all of him. He could never be a mere spectator to its beauties, a critic of its way; he had to live according to its rules, abide by and uphold its codes.

He passed down a bank, up the farther side. He threaded a stand of pines, forded a creek, and came again to the rest of the ridge. The land turned rugged and rocky and after an hour or two he found himself on the far edge of the Rocking Chair range. The ancient icecap had left its scourings here: massive pinnacles of stone, great mounds of granite material thrown about to form odd figures. It was a stretch of country that matured nothing but rattlesnakes and afforded protection only to men like Jere Streeter. But to his kind it was an ideal refuge.

Young Jim was never in doubt as to the renegade's path, for at intervals he saw Jere ahead of him, gradually dropping nearer. It was as if he had meant that young Jim should see him and be drawn on, that he meant to fight it out. When at last young Jim saw him draw up four hundred yards away and wheel about, he knew the man was choosing his ground and casting back on the trail to discover what odds were against him. Then Jere got off his horse and fired a shot, the bullet falling short. After that both horse and man were out of sight.

Young Jim got out of the saddle and left his horse beyond bullet range, himself marching forward without attempt at concealment until he had approached within less than a hundred yards of Jere Streeter's natural barricade.

"If you were looking for the posse, amigo," he muttered, "I hope you're pleased. We'll scrap it alone."

Another shot struck the rocks in front of him. He forged on, stolidly, pressing straight at the renegade. But within fifty yards he swiftly sidestepped and fell behind protection. He heard the renegade mocking him.

"Losing your guts, kid? Come on! I'm here to be took! The buzzards are a-going to have a feed!"

Young Jim rested a moment. This was no ordinary opponent. With all his boasting, his open display of contempt, he would use his canny mind. Not for an instant did young Jim suppose Jere Streeter would wait behind that upthrust wall of rock. He would be sliding around, to one side or the other, trying for a certain shot.

"Now," he murmured, "I think he credits me with some intelligence. He'll probably figure I'll inch ahead in a more or less direct line, because he knows I'm anxious to close up. Therefore he'll try to crawl around closer and drop a shot on my back. But which way will he come? Right or left?"

To the right the rocks formed a series of continuous pockets and barricades. It would be extremely easy for Jere to come along that way. To the left it was less rugged and from it the average man would not be apt to expect trouble. Young Jim, understanding Jere Streeter's trickiness, his feline mind, knew it would be in keeping with the man to choose the less probable way. So, hitching his belt tighter, he swung toward the left and began an infinitely slow advance from depression to depression. One particularly elevated rock behind his new path worried him, as it commanded every move he made. But within ten yards he had dropped into a deeper rut of the rocks and was completely shut off from inspection. He could not be absolutely sure Streeter had not watched him choose his course from this vantage point and he stopped and debated switching toward another point of the compass.

He decided against it, willing to match boldness and eager to come against the man. Young Jim could be cautious only so long as he refused to think of Nan's bruised face and his father's head, pierced with a bullet and dirtied with the clay dust of the Roan Horse road. Then he turned utterly savage and refused to heed the voice of reason. He throttled a desire to rise up and scramble on; all that saved him then was the memory of Jere Streeter's sharp and evil face. The man would pin him down with one bullet and ride away — probably to find his sister and inflict other bruises.

So he stuck to his angling and dodging from shelter to shelter, halting every few feet and laying an ear against the surface of the rocks to listen. He knew this was almost a futile thing to do; Jere Streeter would make no sounds, commit no mistakes. When the man exposed himself it would be to make a kill. Young Jim came to a V-shaped pathway between rocks leading into something like a crater. Gathering his legs beneath his stomach he shot across and downward; and as suddenly leaped backward. The instrument of death had been at his very face, coiling a mottled body and spitting hate from a red mouth and brilliant eyes. Young Jim circled away and left the snake alone.

It left his nerves jangling and he stopped to pull himself together. "Between the two of 'em," he muttered, "I'll be dead of excitement before a shot settles it." The sun stood well above the eastern rim, a flaming forecast of the day's heat. Morning's wind had died and already young Jim saw the shimmering of atmospheric waves rising off the rocks. The sweat rolled down his cheeks and stung his eyes, waking in him a strong desire for water.

Water was tantalizingly near, yet out of reach. In his creeping progression, he had swung close to the borders of Secret River. Ten feet would bring him to a point where he might see the shadowed ribbon of water down below — a drop of thirty feet, not quite sheer, yet steep enough to make a man climb as he would climb a ladder. Young Jim wiped away the beads of sweat and moved to another piece of shelter, from which he commanded a long narrow vista ahead.

It was such an ordeal as he had never before gone through and for all his steady courage he could not prevent the steady constriction of his nerves. It grew to be almost like a neuralgic pain; the nerves of his neck twitched and he found himself looking behind with an increasing frequency. He had reached that pitch which causes men to see and hear things nonexistent. It was one such reaction that sent him clawing for his gun, whereupon he made the startling discovery that he had no gun. Somewhere along his tortured path it had fallen out; he guessed his swift jump away from the snake had capsized it from the holster. The discovery sent his plans a-crashing; yet singularly enough, it steadied him. That very queer thing known as the cold courage of desperation took hold of his nerves, shook him together once more.

"Well, I said I'd break him with my hands. Now I'll do it. Damn the man, where is he?"

Out of the question grew the answer. Rather the hint of an answer. He could lay his senses to no tangible warning; nevertheless there was that same flaring of his instinct to self-preservation, the same prickling of flesh he had known a few hours before when he had stood bound in the Streeter house and felt the presence of Springtime in the room. It is a quality known to all wild animals;

in man it is quiescent through centuries of disuse. Still, it comes to him at certain supreme moments as it came to young Jim. Just beyond him, he was sure, lay Jere Streeter, waiting to strike.

He was so sure of it that he gathered all his muscles, pulled his legs beneath him and prepared to shove himself upward and over the rock that concealed him. That was the power of his warning; on the edge of acting he exerted all of his will to hold himself back and he marshaled all the logic of the situation to persuade himself to stick in his shelter and let the other man act. Yet his muscles grew tense, collecting force for the spring. If Jere Streeter was on the other side of the rock, did the man likewise know that he, young Jim, was within arm's reach? It seemed likely, knowing how abundantly equipped Streeter was with animal instincts. If that were the case, he would be launching himself at the muzzle of a gun. If it were not so, and the renegade hid elsewhere, he would only be exposing himself to fire.

That was as far as he managed to reason. Then he had thrown his big body out of the shelter, up to the top of the rock and down into the adjoining hollow. Here Streeter's slender body sprawled like a reptile on the ground; as he fell, shoulders foremost, he had one flashing view of the man's face, drawn and dry and deadly. The thin lips were drawn back and the beady eyes were stabbing him with hate. Another snake coiled to strike. Young Jim smothered him; a gun exploded, but young Jim felt nothing of the bullet. Swinging round he got hold of the gun, wrenched it free and threw it far over the edge of the cliff. He was struck twice with incredible swiftness and force; the breath came belching out of him and Jere Streeter writhed clear, clawing like a cat.

The man was beyond arm's reach, groping for a rock to smash down on young Jim's skull; young Jim heard the hysterical whistling of Jere's breath and, swinging his feet like the jaws of a vise, he pulled the man down atop him. He was struck again and again before he could bring up his arms and bind them around the renegade's body. He rolled, rose to his knees, at the same time slipping one hand upward to the thin neck. Then they were both on their feet, and Jere had wriggled free and was backing away. He was apparently without bones and joints — nothing but elusive muscle. Once again he bent for a rock, this time securing it. Young Jim dodged and closed in, striking a sledge-hammer blow with all the weight of his body behind it. He felt a snapping, heard a cry; as in some dreadful nightmare he saw the renegade staring at him out of a crooked face, whirl like a top and then vanish from sight.

Young Jim braced his feet wide apart, feeling the hard pounding of his heart. Up in the sky was a blood-red ball of fire seeming to overspread the sky. He shook with a kind of ague and his whole body drooped in weariness and disgust; the killing instinct ran out of him like sand from a funnel. Stepping forward he sent a glance down the sides of the precipice and turned away. One sight was enough. On the way to his horse he got the gun; the rattlesnake was still there, but he had had enough of killing for one day and he left it alone. Stumbling on, he got into the saddle and turned homeward.

"Go along, boy. Secret River's got another secret to sing about. It's a day I don't want to remember."

But the valley was clean from then on of the sinister influence of the Streeters. Never again would men look westward over the ridge and shake their heads in troubled contemplation. An evil growth had been rooted out; the rich rare air would be the cleaner for it, the sun should shine the brighter. The country could go back to its peaceful, humdrum ways.

It was a long somber ride home. Once there he found the posse waiting for him. Going to the bunkhouse, he spoke to a pair of his men. "Ride again, boys. Go over to Secret River bluffs, down to the three ducks. Jere Streeter's there."

Then he started for the house to find Nan. Inside the door he was confronted with the schoolmistress; and with all her short-sightedness, her lack of ability to read this country, she was woman enough to read Jim Bolles at that moment. Read him through and through as he put his hands on the table, dead tired of flesh and of spirit. Nor was the story pleasant to her. Too clearly she saw she could never share this man's life, never claim his loyalty or affection. Perhaps it made her reckless of her words, perhaps it made her unconsciously cruel. Throwing back her head defiantly, her black eyes widening, she spoke in a sharp, satisfied manner.

"You won't find Nan Streeter," she said. "She's gone."

Chapter 6

Young Jim's head fell a little forward; he passed a hand across his eyes, speaking in a slow, soft drawl. "Where did she go?"

"How do I know?" demanded the lady. "I'm not her guardian. She made Springtime hitch the buckboard and take her toward Roan Horse."

Young Jim was nodding; a light flickered and faded in the deep wells of his eyes. "I guess it's the only thing she would do. The only thing she could do. And didn't she say anything — leave any word?"

The schoolmistress watched young Jim for several moments. Perhaps she had read wrong; it might be he would change. But she could find no comfort for her in that tight-set, gaunt and wistful countenance. "She said a few things," admitted the lady. "Oh, yes, your black-haired outlaw woman — "

Young Jim's words fell across the room

like a whiplash. "Madam, don't go beyond the mark!"

" — said something. But first I had a word. What right has she with her past, being that kind of a woman from that kind of a family, to ask shelter of you! What right has she to want your name? Why, she'd be an anchor around your neck. You are one breed. She's another. Yes, I told her that! Of course she wants your name. It would be just like her to want to save herself from all she's got to face!"

"And what did she say?" inquired young Jim in a curiously gentle voice. The knuckles of his fists whitened as he gripped the chair.

The schoolmistress's eyes flared from the memory of that interview. "Tiger woman! She's just that. She stood just where you stand and looked at me! I thought she meant to kill me! Then she said — here's something to flatter your vanity, Jim Bolles — 'I have no claim on him. I'm not worth him. But neither are you. I hope he sees you as I do!' " She flung herself toward the stairs, almost crying. "I'm leaving in the morning! What a horrible, savage land! I never want to see it again. I never will!"

Young Jim ran out of the door and toward the corrals, throwing a word to Joe Tatum. "Joe, you take the prisoners to jail. I have got to go to town — now!" He roped and saddled a fresh horse from the corral and galloped down the Roan Horse road.

He saw Springtime first. Springtime leaning on the hotel porch in town and talking to a middle-aged woman. The puncher saw him come and motioned gravely to the upper part of the hotel. "Room ten," said he. Young Jim went in, walked up the stairs and knocked. He heard a slow voice summon him, and the next moment he faced her.

The young boys were sleeping on the bed and she put a finger up to warn him. "Hush, Jim. They haven't had rest for so long."

The bruises showed on her cheeks; there was pain in her dark eyes. Even so, young Jim thought he had never seen a fairer, finer woman. There was metal in her that no Streeter could claim, a calm fortitude and resolution untainted by the treachery and narrow-mindedness of the Streeter training. Alone of her kind she was straightforward, clear-eyed. Young Jim tried to say something — and failed. In the end he put out his arms.

"Nan," he said, brokenly, "there's the blood of your family on my hands! I can't ask you now! But, by the Lord, I love you!"

"Hush!" Light flickered through the somber shadows of her face. "Jim, what would

I be doing to marry you now? A Streeter and a Bolles! You couldn't carry the load."

"I can carry the world if you're with me! This is the West, Nan. Folks don't harbor malice against you. Tomorrow is another day. As for me — "

She whispered a single word, "Jere — "

He said nothing, but she saw his outstretched hands and she understood. She knew then that never, as long as she lived, would young Jim tell her the whole story. As for him, he saw the mingled pain and relief in her face and he understood that whatever her thoughts might be, she would keep them to herself. They were alike.

"I — I don't hold it against you, Jim," she whispered. "It is better that he is dead. All he has done in this world has caused nothing but grief. Oh, Jim, I'm sorry for you!" Then she came a little closer. "I'm going to Gaskell this afternoon. They want a waitress at the hotel."

"I hate to think of you working — "

She stopped him and something like her old spirit came back. "I've got to do it my own way, Jim. I want to show them I'm straight. I want to feel I'm doing something. I've got my debts to pay."

The very words of his father. He dropped his arms. "Wherever you are, Nan, you know you've got me. You'll always have me. Now or fifty years from now. But I guess there's no hope for me, then?"

She was watching him, seeming to memorize the lines of his gaunt, sober face, the heavy rumble of his voice. For perhaps a minute she was silent. Then:

"Jim, if you feel the same a year from now — "

"I'll feel the same always, Nan."

"Then come and get me when the time is up."

For the first time a slow smile crinkled around his eyes. "This world is worth living in now. Nan, I won't wait a minute over the time. Maybe not that long." He looked wistfully at her, then turned to the door. "Work to be done."

"Wait, Jim!"

He swung back. She came to him and her lips brushed his cheek. "That's to bind you. Lord keep you, until then."

Young Jim groped out of the room and stumbled downstairs. Bright sun drenched the streets and blinded his eyes so that he passed within five feet of Springtime, yet didn't see the puncher. But he heard Springtime's voice and a woman's answer. Going to his horse, he started home.

Dusk was falling on the Rocking Chair;

purple shadows swirled around the buildings and over the yard. A light glimmered from the bunkhouse and the drone of talk floated out from it. Down past the barn came the groan of the gate and the thud of a horse's feet. A shrill yell went rocketing out into the semidarkness as Springtime wheeled a buckboard over the space and stopped at the porch of the big house. He was coming back from Roan Horse and he was not coming alone. Beside him, filling somewhat more than her half of the seat, was the lady he had met on the hotel porch. A lady as old as Springtime and with the determined, assured air of one who had willingly fought the battles of life and perhaps had launched a few conflicts of her own. As the boys came out of the bunkhouse and young Jim stepped on the porch, it was observed by all and sundry that when Springtime handed her down from the buckboard she favored him with a possessive, victorious glance.

Springtime cleared his throat and spread one hand outward. "Introducing Miz Clarabelle Petty. Miz Petty is my affianced bride. As soon as I have collected my possibles and drawn my pay we will return to the civic confines of Roan Horse and have the nuptial ribbons tied in the knot, which, though it may slip, never parts."

"La," said the lady, "what a fool you can make of yourself." She swept the yard with one grim glance. "So this is the outfit you work for?"

"Welcome to Rocking Chair," offered young Jim, coming forward. "You've had a long ride. You are welcome to stay the night, or as long as you please."

"Thanks," said Miz Petty. "I'm accustomed to be treated as a lady and I'll accept with pleasure."

The schoolmistress had come downstairs and now stood framed in the door. Springtime went through the introducing again. Then he stated, in a tone that exuded satisfaction, "My affianced is a schoolma'am. Yep, she's a schoolma'am."

"That is very interesting," said Evelyn Fleming, dryly.

"Interesting?" snorted Miz Petty, sizing up the situation. She was not a dull woman and Springtime's manner with this pretty girl leaning against the door, indicated some kind of private retaliation. "Shucks, it's dull as dishwater. What's interesting about a room full of brats? Any idiot can teach. I did, for ten years and nobody ever put me on a pedestal."

Springtime moved uneasily. "I met Miz Petty purely by accident," he explained. "But

I knowed her over in Robey County a long time ago. We went to school together."

Miz Petty struck him with a deadly glance. "Oh, it wasn't so long ago, either. My stars, you'd think we was old folks."

An oppressive silence fell upon the group. A small sigh seemed to come from the ranks of the bunkhouse crew. Springtime tried again in a jocular vein. "Well, an education sure is a wonderful thing. A man ought to have it. He sure ought. Now, apple blossom, here's a problem in arithmetic which I need help on. If a man is to get fifty dollars a month working in the livery stable, and he owes ten dollars on a poker debt, seven and a half to a bartender, thirty-five on private affairs, how much is a-going to be left for housekeeping? Never mind fractions."

"Hmf!" said Miz Petty. "There won't be any dividing of your check, Povy. I get it each month and I keep it, understand? What is more, if I hear about your gambling or if I smell a drop of liquor on your breath before we are married I shall certainly leave you flat. There's things no lady will tolerate. Mr. Jim, I'll thank you to show me to my chamber."

Young Jim took her in, leaving Springtime a melancholy figure on the porch. The crew began to go away one by one, hurriedly as if something ailed their faces and presently a wild and choking wail emerged from the corral. Young Jim came back and found Springtime wandering moodily across the yard. He put an arm on the puncher's shoulder, speaking gently.

"Listen, Springtime. No man ever played one woman against another and came out with a whole shirt."

"I always knowed there was a catch in this education rigamarole," muttered Springtime. "Well, I promised her I'd run in double harness and that promise stands. Come to think about it, did I pop the question to her, or did she just sort of tamper with my gentlemanly instincts and inch it out of me? Funny, I can't seem to recollect."

"I'll miss you, Springtime."

"Yeah," said Springtime in a muffled voice. He looked up along the bench, his eyes gleaming with the reflection of his cigarette. "Roundup is about due, ain't it? I suppose some damn blacksmith-handed guy will be a-ridin' my string."

Silence. Suddenly the cigarette made a glowing arc in the night and fell with a shower of sparks. "Jim, as a personal favor, will you lend me fifty dollars?"

"Done," said young Jim. "More if you want it."

"No, fifty is ample. It'll be money well spent. Did you hear her say she'd throw me over if I touched cards or drink?"

"The words as she spoke them," agreed young Jim, "were simple and distinct."

"Well, I'm a-going to town in the morning with that fifty and Miz Petty. Twenty of it goes on faro tables. Then I'm going to get so drunk a hog would be ashamed of me. Whichupon I'll stagger under her window by the hotel and sing that song about Annie Gray."

Young Jim moved off. "I'll tell the cook to leave a little for supper for you tomorrow night."

Springtime drew a deep breath. "It's sure queer how man ain't got sense enough to know when he's well off. But no heavy-handed son of a barber is a-going to ride my string." He looked at the vanishing figure of his boss and across his wooden face came something like affection. "It's roundup time."

"I'll be waiting for you, Springtime," said young Jim.

Trail of the Barefoot Pony

Chapter 1

Nothing in all the world is so rich and rare and invigorating as an early fall morning in cattle land; and, when the two partners, Joe and Indigo, stepped from their cabin just at the moment the land was flushing with the promise of a sun down the horizon, they stopped side by side and felt their gaze sweep the little canyon in silence and satisfaction. In the thin air was a winelike pungency that swept away every doubt and every weariness; the pines along the slope held dark pools of night crispness and the needles shimmered with an emerald color they would not again possess during the day.

Not a stone's throw from their door the shallowing river lapped softly against the pebbled beach. Farther up, where it buckled through the gorge, was the subdued murmur and swash of rapids and occasionally a remote boom of some racing jet flaying itself against rock walls. At this distance the sound had the power of soothing and cooling the spirit. Joe's serene eyes studied the scene — river and slope, cabin and barn — and his broad shoulders lifted with a strong inhalation of this bracing air.

Every object standing against the morning light was etched clearly and brought deceptively near by the transparency of the atmosphere; the wisplike columns of smoke eddying from their chimney seemed to stand stiff and still. To a veteran like Joe, who had been almost everywhere and seen almost everything along the thousands of miles of trail, this was the earth's fairest spot.

He turned to the small, shrunken figure by his side and smiled, a smile that illumined the lean features and evoked the full, mellow kindliness of his nature. Small lines sprang about his eyes, lines worn there by many years of looking far across the rolling leagues into the sun. His temples were beginning to silver.

A soft chuckle welled up from his throat and passed into the still air.

"You're in a bad hole now, Indigo. This is a busted-down puncher's paradise and you've got to admit it. Even a skinny little buzzard of disaster like you has got to agree. Think hard. Try to find something wrong.

You can't do it. It ain't possible. Ever since I was a kid and took the out trail from Abilene I've been looking for a place to light and rest. This is it, Indigo."

Indigo's thin, shrewish face brooded over a cigarette and his pale orbs stabbed the landscape as if to capture something objectionable, something that augured grief. Such was the nature of the diminutive, dynamic, fighting bantam. Life had been harsh to Indigo, nor had he ever made any attempt to let it deal kindly with him. He always met trouble halfway and sometimes seven-eighths of the way; and it was a point of pride with him never to admit anything was exactly right. But on this morning, as on the other six mornings of their joint occupancy of the twenty-acre homestead in the canyon, he went down to defeat. All he said was, "Yeah, it's pretty nice. I guess it'll do." Reluctantly he said it, his saturnine, angular cheeks implying mental reservations. As far as Indigo was concerned there was a catch in all good things and there must be a catch, consequently, in this.

"Well," decided Joe, "we'd better get going. Sooner we wind up the purchase of this place the happier I'll feel about it. Henry Bonnick might die on us before we pay him."

"Yeah, he's prob'ly changed his mind and

won't sell," grunted Indigo. "Or we'll get sick and have to use the money on doctoring. Or else we'll lose it on the road."

"Feeble," said Joe, grinning. "Awful feeble. When you get to carping on little items like that it means you're stumped for trouble. Let's go."

They saddled and turned past the cabin, leaving the door wide open and a pot of beans bubbling on a dying fire. The very first hour of residence in the cabin had brought them grief with certain tough gentlemen around the hills and they were not sure the cabin would not be ransacked between departure and return; but a lifetime's schooling in Western etiquette would not allow them to close or lock the door of any domicile of theirs. So they proceeded leisurely along the river's bank, southbound to the county seat at Smoky River with the full intent of paying to one Henry Bonnick the sum of four hundred dollars, which was his set price on land and improvements. One week ago they had met this Henry Bonnick under duress and strain. He had turned the property over to them and fled to avoid further collision with the tough gentlemen of the hills, asking the partners to come into Smoky River and pay him, thereby insuring himself against carrying such a sum of money through a forlorn and debatable territory.

As the partners traveled, the canyon walls subsided and eventually the trees fell behind. They rode out upon a flat, undulating land without break or flaw for many monotonous miles. Away east were the spire points of a range against which the first full red rays of the sun broke and glared. And at the touch of that dull, molten ball the crisp spice of the air collapsed. An oppressive shield of heat settled down by degrees, the dust rose up to sting nostril and eye, and the sombreros of Joe and Indigo tipped lower. The trail led arrow straight to the southern reaches, but the river bowed away while the banks narrowed and the water was absorbed into the arid soil. Another twenty miles would make of it a brackish rivulet in which the gaunt cattle would stand hoof deep.

"We've got to see about getting some peach trees and strawberry plants for our place," mused Joe. "They'll bear in two-three years. I always did have a yearning to assume the Biblical attitude of reclining under my own fig bush."

"I'm going to stock up on cartridges," croaked Indigo. "Which ain't so Biblical, mebbe, but considerable more practical. Somebody coming, 'way off yonder."

An imperceptible dust bomb rose along the course of their path. A great deal short of it was a house and a windmill; a great deal beyond it was the faint cleavage of horizon that marked a town. The partners, being old hands and having ridden many miles together, forebore speaking. Speech was often an aggravation, while silence never rubbed anybody's nerves.

So, sunk in their own reveries, the partners plodded ahead, watching the dust bomb as a matter of diversion. It died away at the end of a half hour, by which they gathered the traveler had reached the ranch house. A little later it resumed and grew larger, swelling directly toward them. Meeting strangers on the rail was always an event and, in barren country like this, sometimes a surprise. Therefore Indigo began hitching up his gunbelt long before the time of meeting and now and then casting a darkly suggestive glance at his partner. But Joe's calm cheeks never changed out of a graven expression, nor did his easy carriage shift perceptibly The blue eyes, half shuttered against the violent light, clung to the advancing traveler and the wide lips were thoughtfully pursed.

Horse and rider emerged from the glare of the distance. A little later a fragment of metal gear flashed diamond-bright. Yard by yard the narrowing foreground gave up additional facts. A leggy horse and a quite tall rider in a flaring sombrero. The horse was yellowish gray and star-chested, the man gray with dust and riding with a striking stiffness of body, neckpiece and open vest flapping to the beast's motion. Joe's casual yet searching eyes caught the luxury of the saddle with its fine tooling and inlay; he caught also the expensive look of the clothes the man wore.

But, with less than twenty feet intervening, his attention snapped to a far more engrossing fact. This man's holster sat low, with the side of it cut farther down than usual; the gun within it rested rather high, butt and hammer well exposed; and the point of the holster was cut away to allow a free channel for firing while the weapon was still seated. Then the stranger had turned broadside, gun arm away from the partners. This was a politeness and a carefulness not lost on either Joe or Indigo. They reined in and likewise drew about.

"How," said the man in a dry, level voice.

Joe Breedlove was schooled to impassivity when the occasion called for that, yet there was a distinct sharpening of glance as he paid the stranger strict attention. Over the years Joe had seen them come and seen them go, all kinds of men, good, bad or indifferent; men with flaring courage, men without a grain of sand. Experience long ago had taught him better than to classify people too strictly, nor ever to judge too swiftly. But, as he sat there studying, he knew he had at last crossed trails with an individual who was almost a perfect and finished representative of one particular breed. Upon the unusually tall and spare framework of the stranger were certain indelible signs that told him — and warned him.

The fellow was built like a long slice out of a straight tree; there was no give to him, no play. His arms were all hands and his hands all fingers; supple and destructive fingers. The face, as gray as alkali dust, was a series of sharp lines, verging from jaw hinge to a small chin. A dab of sandy brow overlaid two eye slits out of which emerged a lusterless gleam. A thin nose with pinched-in nostrils guarded lips so compressed as to have no curve to them at all; a flat-faced, flat-chested man whose veins seemed withdrawn to the deep interior of his being, thus making him appear bloodless, heatless. Joe was not deceived by that. Here was a man of unusual physique and mentality, untiring, passively grim, able to withstand the urge of sleep or hunger for great lengths of time, and without humor.

Joe heard Indigo moving restlessly in the saddle and by that he knew his partner felt something of the same reaction and threat. So he ducked his head calmly. "Howdy. Tolerable weather."

"In case you're strangers," said the man with the smallest trace of inflection, "it's hot the farther south you go in this country. Right warm in Smoky River."

"We were wondering," drawled Joe, "is Henry Bonnick still in town."

"You'll find him in the stable, chewing straw," droned the man. "Hear tell he's a little nervous about his neighbors up yonder."

"We're taking over his place," said Joe, and felt Indigo's inquiring eye. "Neither of us quite so excitable over bushes rustling around the back door."

"I judge," murmured the man. Joe gathered the idea that there was a slight withdrawal of civility in the fellow's eyes, though he wasn't sure. There was, however, an increase of lip pressure.

"Smoky River is mebbe a good town to do business in," suggested Joe.

The man's gaze opened to a full, hard inspection.

"Folks over at Plaza San Felipe might argue the point."

"Argument," drawled Joe, "is the original sin the book talks about." Usually Joe pronounced his innate philosophy with a genial break of countenance. There was no such change here; his features were on guard. "I have seen argument and done some little arguing. But personally, peace is my motto — until convinced the other fellow don't care much for mottoes."

"I judge," said the man and let the threads of conversation fall flat to the ground. The lull grew pronounced, one man waiting the other out. Indigo began to shift and sigh. The stranger lifted the reins and said, "*Adios,*" in the same chestless tone. The horse beneath him bunched, swirled and was away, moving with a stiffness of forefeet that appeared to be caught from the ramrod posture of the rider. Joe and Indigo moved on, neither deigning to look back. A quarter mile later Indigo's querulous question broke the silence.

"Why spill our business to him? I didn't like that jasper. Made me mad just to look at him. Made me nervous and hostile. He's just the kind of a shad-bellied, gimlet-eyed duck that reminds me of a diamondback. What'd you tell him anything for?"

It was a considerable interval before Joe

answered, and Indigo, casting a glance at his partner, was nearly shocked at the tall, easy-going man's change of expression. Joe had on his fighting face for no apparent reason at all, which in itself augured some tremendous upset to his feelings, for Joe rarely dignified any man or any occasion with the full weight of his wrath. Finally he met Indigo's curious look with hard, troubled eyes.

"Thought it wise to announce ourselves," he muttered.

"He don't look like the gossiping kind," stated Indigo, "if it was your intention to spread our designs to the whole county."

"No. Just wanted him to know. Just him, personal. He's the type of a fellow I have met three-four times in my life, Indigo. Bad."

Indigo, being agreed with, experienced one of his celebrated changes of opinion. "Oh, maybe he ain't so tough. I never saw the fellow yet that needed more'n one bullet in the right spot. He wasn't pointing any fingers at us, anyhow."

But Joe shook his head and reached for his cigarette papers, visibly struggling to right himself. "I'm a damned fool, Indigo. Acted like a six-year school kid. I can get along with almost anybody in the world. I can grin at any sort of trouble and find good in blamed near any sort of mortal. But when I run across a man without heart or nerves and with eyes like he had and ears like he had — did you observe they was twice as small as any ordinary fellow's and as flat against his head as a sheet of paper? — and when I know in my bones he is a better man than I am in muscle and speed, I go tight all over. I can't help it. Something inside just rises up like a snake's tail and begins to rattle. Nine times out of ten he could beat me to the draw or break my back, and yet I want to meet up with him and try it out. It's like a fever. Twice in my life it's happened. I'm the worst fool on God's green footstool, but there is one kind of a gent I'm afraid of and can't live in peace with. That's him, Indigo."

Indigo lifted his scrawny shoulders. "He'll pass on. Won't cross our trail."

But Joe, reversing the usual relation between them issued a sober prophecy. "It's in the cards I'll have to fight that man. Always happens like that."

There was nothing under the sun that Indigo feared and nobody he reverenced with the exception of Joe, and it upset him to hear his partner admitting the superiority of any other human. Muttering under his breath, he stared all around the horizon and fixed his jade orbs on a dim trailer of dust in the direction of the peaks. He called Joe's attention and both of them studied it carefully.

"Looks like that fellow made a big circle and is trying to beat us into Smoky River," judged Indigo. "Big hurry for such a hot day. Why?" Suddenly he turned fretful. "The mystery in this doggone country is heavy enough to cut with a cheese knife. I'm beginning to feel chills up my spine, which has meant trouble ever since I was a little kid and fell off the barn roof. I wish folks would let us alone."

They bore down on the windmill and ranch house. A great oak towered in the yard of the house and a long rope was affixed to a branch, from which was suspended a water bag swaying with the imperceptible movement of the air. Being thirsty pilgrims, the partners drew in by it. Joe, punctilious to the marrow, lifted his voice at the house and waited patiently. Presently the door opened and a girl stood uncertainly on the threshold, watching them out of gray, troubled eyes. Chestnut hair rippled in the sunlight and a clear oval face turned from partner to partner. Joe's hat came off at a wide sweep.

"Do you mind, ma'am, if we draw a drink?"

"Help yourself."

They took turns at the spigot, and got back a-saddle. Joe, conscious all the while of a reserve in the atmosphere, felt it incumbent on him to offer a mild explanation. "A dusty ride out of the hill country. My partner and me, not knowing the country, didn't think to bring canteens."

The girl inclined her head, accepting it soberly. "I thought possibly you might be from Plaza San Felipe. Though none of that outfit would ask leave before drinking."

That was all. The door closed, the partners pressed on while the heat grew more and more intense. Smoky Hill alternately swelled and diminished through the burnished fog. Man and beast were touched by it; leather and metal turned scorching hot.

"She's afraid of something," was Indigo's laconic comment. "Afraid of Plaza San Felipe folks. Second time you and me has heard the name mentioned. Must be the home of that original sin you mentioned."

"That fellow with the dead face just passed through here a little before us, remember," said Joe. "That's what made her afraid. A comely girl out here alone. It ain't right. And where's all the punchers you'd expect to find on an outfit that size?"

"Hell has took a holiday, I guess," croaked

Indigo, wilting farther beneath the umbrella proportions of his sombrero.

Mile after mile they put behind them in sultry silence. Smoky River became something more than a deceptive promise on the horizon. They passed an abandoned wagon, they passed a flaring sign regarding the excellences of a hotel: "The Western Empress — Every Room With A Window And A Mattress." Corrals marched by, deep in dust; the river came back from its tortuous progress through the burning desolation and they crossed its inch-deep surface on a covered bridge that rumbled a fanfaronade of their entry to the county seat. A single street passed between beaten, paint-scaled buildings and dwindled into the yonder desert. One forlorn, gaunt brick edifice flaunted a scarred announcement on its walls, years old: "Lotta Crabtree And A Glorious Galaxy — " The rest was abraded out. Adjoining was a watering trough, toward which the partners pointed, going past it and on into the grateful gloom of a livery stable's vault. A dozen men, more or less, lounged around, and in the background Joe saw the up-tilted face of Henry Bonnick. He lifted a casual arm at the fellow and slid from his pony.

"Well, friend, the week is up and here we are."

Henry Bonnick exhibited strangely mixed emotions. He flashed a glance from the silent group to the partners, as if conveying a desire for secrecy. Tolerating this bizarre behavior, Joe and Indigo strolled on back of the loungers, Bonnick trailing. Beyond earshot, Joe turned to the man.

"Well, we're here and ready to buy. Guess that won't hurt your feelings any."

"I dunno," was Bonnick's dubious answer. "God knows I want to git away, but I guess the deal is off. I don't dare sell."

"Why not?" challenged Indigo. Originally the small man hadn't been so enthusiastic about purchasing the Bonnick place, but this sudden opposition served to throw his cross-grained nature on the opposite side of the fence. Joe smiled.

"I been told not to sell," grumbled Bonnick. "I been warned."

"I always heard tell," snapped Indigo, "that this was a free country for men over voting age."

"Yeah? Mebbe you'll learn more about these parts if you stay."

"Always willing to learn," observed Joe. "Who seems to be the ace-high gent in the case?"

Bonnick looked about him and lowered his voice.

"Don't say a word to nobody, but Slash LeGore got wind I was selling out. About half an hour ago he comes in and says it'd be better if I didn't encourage new settlers thataway."

"Who's this high-binding sucker?" challenged Indigo. "The deal's going through and I'd like to see him stop it!"

Joe's face, meanwhile, had settled and sobered. He touched Bonnick's shoulder.

"This LeGore would be a tall fellow with a gray face and little flat ears?"

"Pick out the hardest egg you ever saw," muttered Bonnick. "That would be LeGore."

"I thought so," drawled Joe and he switched his glance to Indigo. There was again a tightening of his features. "That's our friend with the dead face. Didn't I say it was in the cards I'd collide with him?"

Chapter 2

Joe Breedlove, looking thoughtfully down the stable, observed that the loiterers up front were quite silent and paying more than casual attention to this scene. Indigo, however, was lecturing Bonnick with a rousing irate pitch to his voice, entirely unaware of any such subtleties of atmosphere. The small partner's enormous appetite for unpopular or dangerous cases was at the moment feeding in lush pastures. There was nothing Indigo detested more than to see one man put unfair pressure on another. Being but a shadow and a carcass himself he had always been extremely sensitive about infringement of personal rights.

A larger individual had to look only once on Indigo with doubt to find the bantam swarming over him; furthermore, his sensitiveness extended to all manner and forms of real or alleged injustice which in no way concerned him. It didn't have to be Indigo's quarrel, nor did he need much of an invitation to enter on the weak side and do holy battle. Insofar as violence, mayhem and sudden death were concerned, Indigo had a strong sense of proprietorship in the human race.

"Who," he grunted, pale orbs turning to an even paler emerald, "is this mug, Slash LeGore? What call has he got to be giving anybody orders? You owe him anything, beholden to him, related to him, marry any of his sisters?"

"Nothing and none," muttered Henry Bonnick, spurred by his jangled nerves. "You wouldn't ask that question if you'd lived here about a week. Slash LeGore is Slash LeGore."

"Got a personal following, uh?" pressed Indigo. "Folks think he's high, low, jack and the game?"

Out of a distressed soul Bonnick resorted to homemade adjectives. "Saul's lost kingdom! You bet he's got a personal following. But not a following of decent men, mister. Oh, you'll see!"

"Where's he hole up?"

"Plaza San Felipe is his private honkytonk. It's his town. Anything he touches belongs to him. You'll see."

"And you're not disposed to sell?" interposed Joe.

Henry Bonnick almost wrung his hands. "It ain't that I don't want to shuffle the dust of this country off my boots! But it is a long ride to the railroad, friend. And Slash LeGore'd know I turned it over to you before I saddled a horse."

"Gave no reasons, did he?"

"LeGore don't give anybody reasons."

"Think it over," suggested Joe. "If you want company riding to that railroad, we'll supply it."

"Yeah," muttered Bonnick and turned back. Abreast of the small crowd he collected himself sufficiently to make a general introduction. "Boys, these fellows are all right. Strangers in the country, but they didn't come from the east."

"What's east which ain't so good?" Indigo wanted to know.

"Plaza San Felipe," retorted Bonnick, and such was the state of his mind that he ambled into the blazing sun and through the middle of the street, neglecting the fragment of shade along the north walk.

"Fourth time we've heard of that town," mused Joe.

Every man in the stable wore a gun. Beyond a bale of hay stood a line of rifles. It wasn't the heat only that drove them in here; they acted like people waiting for something to happen. Indigo growled a phrase about being hungry, so they turned out of the place, vainly trying to walk in the thin shade. Henry Bonnick had already disappeared, leaving the partners alone on a sultry, empty thoroughfare.

Tension hung over the town, as oppressive and stifling as the accumulating temperature of the lengthening afternoon. In the dead silence they heard the clack and jingle of their own bootsteps rise into distant and sluggish echoes.

Joe shook his head. "Too hot to eat steak and onions, Indigo. Beer and crackers is our style. Let's hit that saloon across the stem. Lift your eyes to the second story of this village."

Right above them was a window overlooking a slight balcony. The sash was up and a rifle lay balanced across the sill while a man in shirtsleeves looked down with a sweat-swollen face. Second-floor rooms were nothing less than purgatories on an afternoon like this; yet the partners, following the original discovery, made note of other windows raised and other men staring out. Indigo's skinny frame stiffened with an electric excitement.

"We're right smack into something about to begin to commence, Joe. Say, let's get that lunch over with before the chivaree begins. I do better on a full stomach."

"We're keeping strictly out of this," Joe warned him.

They pushed into the saloon and into a gloom made by drawn shutters. A crowd, slightly larger than the one over at the stable, sat around the walls, neither playing cards nor drinking. The partners received the full force of a mass inspection as they sauntered to the bar and called for liquid ease. Indigo, who took such intent scrutiny with bad grace always, began to mutter, but Joe shook his head and drank his beer. By and by his blue eyes twinkled and he shot a drawling question at the barkeep. "Tax collector coming to town or are you boys trying to keep out an attack of spotted fever?"

The barkeep shook his head and maintained a glum silence. Indigo moved to the free lunch and sorted out enough sandwiches to supply a basket social. The doors opened, letting in a pair of men and a momentary glow of yellow, torpid light. One of the two was Henry Bonnick and when he discovered the partners drinking he turned to the quiescent citizens as if he had just remembered a necessary explanation. "Those fellows are all right. I know 'em to be responsible." Then he brought the other man over to Joe.

"Want you should meet Sheriff Foshay, friend."

Joe stretched out his long arm to the sheriff and gravely announced himself, at the same time drawing Indigo into the ceremony. The sheriff was a pleasant fellow with anxious eyes, but he acknowledged the partners with a distinct reserve.

"Henry," he said, "tells me you're traveling up from the south?"

Joe, feeling that he and Indigo were under suspicion, adopted frankness. "Batwing was our last stop, but we wintered on the Triangle S Bar near Three Falls."

The sheriff wrinkled his brow. "Let's see — that would be Bill Farow's place, wouldn't it?"

"No. Jim Gaines's. Clubfoot Rhine, foreman." Joe knew the sheriff was only pretending unfamiliarity to test him. The official's manner became more friendly and he motioned at the barkeep.

"Another one. Well, I'm always glad to see new men here. Staying long maybe?"

"Depends," was Joe's noncommittal answer. He looked at Bonnick.

"I told him," explained Bonnick in a low voice. "I'd tell Sheriff Foshay anything."

The sheriff's gravity deepened. "It ain't for me to say what you boys ought to do.

Like to see you stick to the region. At the same time I'll have to admit you're running into a dangerous sort of situation. Maybe you know?"

"We see a lot of artillery," agreed Joe. "And we've gathered something about a town called Plaza San Felipe."

The sheriff drank his beer; a slow-moving, thoughtful man, transparently honest and struggling to be fair all around. "This town," he observed, "has been county seat for fifty-six years. Once it was a great town, as you can judge." He pointed to the walls of the saloon where hung a series of paintings. "Those were the fast boom days of Smoky River. It's just a cow town now, dying on its feet. When we was big, the Plaza wasn't anything but one 'dobe hut where rustlers lived. Miners came into the hills yonder and Plaza has grown to be a live place. They want the county seat. Last election the question came up and they lost it. But — " and he stressed the words — "they still want it."

"It's still a hangout of rustlers and gun fanners," interjected Bonnick. "It's Slash LeGore's own — "

"I will say nothing about that," cut in the sheriff. "It ain't my place to speak ill of any section or any man." He studied Joe for a long interval. "You can read the story with your own eyes, friend. Trouble may come which ain't any of your making. Why should you get mixed in it? Better stay clear. All the boys are a little nervous, but I hope it'll blow over. Glad I met you gents, and call on me for any help I can be."

He went out, trailed by Bonnick. A horse drummed down the street, setting up a confused excitement within the saloon; then a young chap with a scorched dust-caked face came panting in. "Nobody," he announced, "can get near the Plaza. But I saw across the roof tops from the side hill. Horses and men, lots of 'em. They'll be coming. You bet they'll be coming!"

Sullen discontent swirled through the room, yet to Joe it seemed the fighting spirit of Smoky River was dampened by a pervading fear. Indigo, always quick to sense such a weakness, snorted his plain disgust. "What kind of a sheepherders' hangout is this?" Then, slapping down the remnant of a sandwich, he lifted his crowing voice. "Let 'em come! Hell's full of such proud and foolish jaspers!"

"Speak big, don't you?" sneered the bearer of bad tidings.

"Me?" countered Indigo with a honeyed politeness. "Son, I was chased out of my first county about the time you changed to cow milk. I've seen many a Sodom in the desert grow proud — and get knocked over by a handful of serious-minded men. This Plaza San Felipe sings a tune as old as the hills."

"Come on," said Joe. "You made your speech."

They passed into the slanting heat, went over to the doubtful shade of the hotel porch and sat down. A solitary townsman reclined half asleep in a rocker at the far end of the porch, but Joe was too preoccupied to notice him more than casually. Indigo, plunged into the tangled affairs of the town, didn't even see the fellow. With all his temperamental shortcomings, Indigo was a strategist of the first water, a master tactician in prairie warfare. His jade orbs slashed here and there, his hatchet jaw achieved a sharp pointedness.

"These fellows are doing it all wrong," he finally protested. "If these Plaza men are as mean as they say, then they won't hit this village by way of the bridge. They'd be fools to frame themselves thataway. They'll ford the river out a ways and ride down from the back side. And we're too scattered about these buildings. We'll interfere with our own fire. We ought to get organized quick."

"What's this 'we' business?" grunted Joe. "When did you buy a stack in this game?"

"I suppose," said Indigo, highly sarcastic, "you'll sit back and let Plaza shoot the lights out of this town? Ain't you able to see the downright meanness of that sink of iniquity?"

"It ain't our quarrel," insisted Joe.

"Supposing this LeGore comes along?"

Joe had no ready answer. He shook his head, staring thoughtfully into the thick, intolerable glare. The unobtrusive man in the porch corner rose and walked away, giving them a single raking glance from beneath a black, scarred sombrero. Joe caught the outline of a blunt, broken-featured visage and was somehow lifted out of his reverie by the sight of it. He looked closer, but the man's back was toward him and the twisted outline of a long practiced rider. A fanfaronade on the bridge warned Smoky River again and a girl, the girl of the lonely ranch, came riding in, stopped before the stable and bent from the saddle.

"Dad in there?"

Sheriff Foshay appeared from an opposite store; the girl dismounted on the shady side, face stamped with concern. They were undoubtedly father and daughter, possessing the same stamp of honesty and simplicity. She was talking to him in swift and subdued words, accenting them with gestures of a small doubled fist. Foshay smiled and kept shaking his head. Thus occupied, they both walked into the store.

Henry Bonnick appeared from another angle, climbed the hotel porch and looked about him. "I've decided to sell," he announced in an ill-controlled whisper. "Then I aim to run like hell! Come on. I've got it all fixed."

He towed the partners rapidly across the street and up a stairway that seemed like a furnace flue. They went into one of the town's sweltering second-story rooms. A fat man in a seersucker suit, glistening with his own grease, waited there with a set of papers on his desk. Henry Bonnick talked with a rapid fire accent.

"I want this done fast. Property's good. Never held a mortgage in my time. Taxes paid. Abstract clear. Read it if you got to, but don't waste no time."

Joe looked once at Indigo and, finding plain assent on his partner's cheeks, reached for a pen. Bonnick had already signed. Joe wrote his own even, angular signature and passed it to Indigo who scratched out something nearly undecipherable. Four hundred dollars changed hands. The lawyer blotted away small pools of sweat, affixed a witnessing signatures and mumbled something about getting the second witness later. He passed the papers around to proper ownership, kept the deed and stood up in the suffocating, miserable cubbyhole with the gesture of one who had stayed under water beyond the limits of human endurance.

"Let's get out of here before we melt. I'll have this recorded right away. See you at the hotel."

Down in the street Bonnick lifted his weatherbeaten face, for the first time mirroring a small shred of wistfulness. He twitched at the sound of a man walking along the boards and shuffled his own feet restlessly from side to side. "It's been my home for a good many years, friends. Can't say I'm awful pleased to go. But it takes a young man to tough it out in this country. I got a son in Nebraska. I'm going there." He paused a moment, then tacked on an awkward request. "I sort of wish you'd drop me a card this fall. Address it to me at Hastings. Just mention if the fish is running well on the Smoky and if that old gray lobo comes down through the canyon. It'd sort of gimme something to think about."

"Sure," agreed Joe with a sudden gruffness. "Want us to ride to the railroad with you?"

Bonnick rejected the offer quickly enough. "It'd attract undue attention. I'm wasting time now. Well, so long. It's a nice little place I sold."

Joe lowered his voice.

"Who's that fellow over there with the broken nose and the black hat?"

Bonnick didn't even turn. Yet his shoulders twitched a little and the fear rose to cloud his eyes.

"Nig Gilpin. Oh, hell, I got to go before it's too late! And don't trust ev'body in this town. It ain't all of them that's fighting for Smoky River. Nobody knows who's acting as ears for LeGore. So long."

He hurried away, vanished in the stable and presently came spurring out. The bridge drummed his departure; momentarily he appeared on the far bank, then curved around the blind side of Smoky River and disappeared. Joe, looking back to observe Gilpin, found the man had melted from the scene.

It was now around four o'clock, with the day's heat at the maximum point. The tropical intensity of it did queer things to man's vision and man's blood; visible sheets of atmosphere rose upward, the building walls stung the hands when touched, and those who found it necessary to be abroad walked with an exaggerated deliberation. Yet as the partners returned to the hotel porch, they felt the increasing strain of anticipation hovering over Smoky River.

Sheriff Foshay came out of the store with his daughter and apparently tried to send her home; at least, his hand rose once toward the bridge. But she shook her head, whereat the sheriff called across to the stable. A red-headed young man with a butternut shirt ambled over, took a short part in the conference and entered the store with the girl. Foshay disappeared into the stable.

"They're coming!"

It had the effect of a bomb. The saloon door belched men, every alley and aperture disgorged them, all aiming for the stable. A woman stepped from a dwelling house and lifted a wailing cry. "Jim — Jim Styles, you come here!" There were other family men in the town who broke from the mêlée and ran toward adjacent houses. Some excitable individual began tolling the church bell, for what reason Joe couldn't understand, and an equally headless fellow fired aimlessly out of a second-story window. The sheriff stepped from the stable and thundered a warning.

"Stop that business, you dam' fool! This ain't no time to go batty! Crowd in here a minute, everybody. I want to say something."

Indigo cast an inquiring glance at Joe. "How about it?"

Joe shook his head. "We keep out of it — as long as we can. I don't doubt we'll have to choose sooner or later, but the Lord hates a premature man. We've got to have some better excuse than idleness to dabble in this. I'm a little sorry for Sheriff Foshay. That's all. Who's to say whether Plaza or Smoky River is best off with the county seat?"

"Hell!" snorted Indigo. "You're a fine specimen to say that. You've wet your feet in trouble on less excuse before now."

Joe sighed. There was a long interval before he answered. "I know it. But I feel it in my bones. I'll be tangled up with LeGore before so very long, Indigo. It's a hunch that grows on me. And I aim to lie back and not do a tap that'll give my conscience room to say I started the argument."

The sheriff addressed the assembled crowd so strongly that the backwash of his words reached the partners: "Boys, it looks like trouble. You stick to your guns and your places. But I don't want a man to let a hammer fall before I've talked with that bunch. I don't want you to make any untoward move, don't want you to give them any ground to start shooting. What they're doing is unlawful, but that don't make it right for us to be unlawful. I'll talk 'em out of it if I can. If I can't, then we've got to resist, and God help us all."

The last phrase rang solemnly through the street. Joe nodded, his fine eyes lighting. "There's a man, a great man. Wherever he goes he'll answer at the head of the roll. It's him that's keeping this town on a level keel."

The crowd split. Foshay was telling off groups to go one place or another, giving each a last warning. Presently he came by the hotel and seeing the partners, checked his stride. "It's not your argument, boys. Better leave town or get out of sight. I'll feel responsible if anything happens to you."

"We'll stay," drawled Joe, "but we won't lift a hand unless — " and the tall partner waved an indefinite arm. The sheriff studied Joe. The both of them were of a type. They understood each other and at first look respected each other. All that they stood for was visible; it lay in Joe's serene eyes and it was stamped on Foshay's rugged, honest cheeks.

"Unless what?" asked Foshay.

"Unless," murmured Joe, "LeGore makes

a personal move against me I'll discount the fact he's warned me, through Bonnick, to stay out of the country. I want no truck with him, but if he pleases to meet me and make a direct challenge, I'll have to answer back."

"A man's got to do as he sees," responded the sheriff gravely, and went on.

The weaklings and faint-hearted were pulling out. From time to time as the late afternoon wore on individual horsemen crossed the bridge and disappeared along the rolling desert. The tension increased. Men came out of their coverts and paced the street to relieve strained nerves and went back again. A flat-bed wagon, carrying a whole family, careened by the hotel while a hatless driver stood up and lashed the horses with the rein ends. The bank doors closed, the shutters went down. Shades dropped on the dwelling windows.

The sheriff had repassed the hotel, accompanied by the young fellow with the red hair and butternut shirt. Next to the store stood the largest building in town with a sign chiseled in a stone façade above the door: COURTHOUSE — 1888. The sheriff and the red-headed youth turned here and superintended some kind of a barricade being erected inside. In sharp contrast with all this preparation the barkeep stood in the saloon doors across the way and propped them open; and six o'clock came to Smoky River, announced by the clang of the restaurant triangle.

Indigo had endured this as long as his nature would allow. He had to move about or blow up. So he suggested supper. Together they ambled east on the street and sat up to an otherwise empty counter. They ordered and ate while the restaurant man, who had the pouchy, mournful jowls of a bloodhound, waited dispiritedly for business that never came. He beat on the triangle a second time and returned.

"The trouble with this town," he announced, "is it don't eat enough beef. Takes meat to build up a man. I eat a pound of steak every meal — do I look like I was afraid of any sucker from Plaza? Why is folks in Plaza so full of meanness and rambunction? Because they's all rustlers and they eat what they rustle. You bet. I guess I got to go out and drum up business if — "

Joe's fork poised. Indigo sprang back from his stool, pale eyes glittering. There was a rhythmic murmur along the hard earth; a yell sailed past the door. "They're coming!" The restaurant man ran toward his door to shut it, but Indigo knocked him back and stood on the threshold, looking both ways on the street.

"Didn't I tell you, Joe, they'd come the back way? That's it, all right."

Joe threw a dollar on the counter. "Do you see the sheriff, anywhere?"

"He's down by the courthouse, standing on the steps."

"Then let's get to the hotel porch and stick there."

They hurried back, hearing the restaurant door slam behind. The sheriff's daughter stood on the hotel porch, trying not to cry, while the red-headed youth awkwardly reassured her and cast an eager glance toward the courthouse. He wanted to be over there, that was plain, and finally he broke away. The girl threw a suddenly suspicious look at the partners and started to follow the redhead. Joe stepped in front of her, gently shaking his head.

"Don't believe your dad would want that, ma'am," he murmured.

"Who are you?" she demanded. "Isn't there anybody in Smoky River besides my father who's got courage enough to stand up and face those cut-throats? Let me go!"

"Your dad has got enough on his hands," said Joe. "Now don't you add to his worries. Just go inside and wait."

The men of the town were running in all directions in spite of having long before posted themselves at certain spots. Doors slammed, a confused shouting rocketed between walls, parties went plunging by the hotel. Above all this turmoil soared Sheriff Foshay's calm voice. "Take it easy, boys. Get set somewhere and don't give any cause for gunplay. I'll handle this." About a dozen of the more stubborn souls ran up the steps and ranged themselves beside him.

Of a sudden the town quivered with the beat of fast traveling ponies; a strong party, riding close and sure, swept along the street, the metal of their gear and guns flashing in the last slanting rays of the westering sun. Joe watched them between half-shut eyes, his tall body as still and straight as the post beside which he loitered. There was an arrogance, a certainty about the Plaza group that instantly angered him. They did this too well. Onward they galloped, now and then a horseman wheeling from the column and taking station beside some door or some alley. Then they were abreast of the hotel, and the dust of the street rose in yellow clouds as they came to a sliding halt. The broken-nosed, cruel-faced Nig Gilpin rode out from the compact body and shook his fist at Sheriff Foshay.

"Well," he rumbled, "here I am. Didn't expect to see me in such good company, huh? Don't reco'nize the top hand which used to work on your ranch, I suppose? Here I am, Bill Foshay, singing a bigger tune."

"It is company I knew you'd go with, first chance, Nig," said Foshay. The sheriff seemed to grow straighter in the emergency of the moment; his dogged face never varied, his command never faltered. "I have seen you going bad a long while. Do you know what you're doing? Do you see — "

"To hell with that!" broke in Gilpin. "We got no time for sermons. You know what we want, don't you? Know what we aim to do, uh? Stand aside, you and the rest of them there jack rabbits."

"Your party, is it?" queried the sheriff.

"You know whose party it is," grunted Gilpin. "But I'm giving orders right at the present time. Stand aside."

"This is the legal county courthouse. This is the duly established county seat. Any man who willfully breaks into the records here is guilty of a misdemeanor. Any man who pulls a gun and starts shooting this afternoon is guilty of starting a riot. Any one of you who begins violence that results in death is guilty of murder! Murder means hanging for any one of you or every man in the party. I'm telling you to cool off and go home."

"Yeah?" muttered Gilpin.

He swung in the saddle and stared at the members of his party stationed along the street. He lifted his eyes to the windows above, to the saloon's open door and the stable's yawning mouth. In passing, his hard eyes brushed the partners, and a malicious grin broke the irregular ugliness of his countenance. Silently he indicated the weak spots of the town and a part of the group broke away, filing here and there. Saloon and stable were covered. Guns lifted toward certain second-story windows. Gilpin squared his shoulders and glowered at the sheriff.

"We got this town hipped, Foshay. You know it. It's up to you. Stand aside and let us rip this courthouse apart or else stand ready for trouble. Smoky River's been dead so long it stinks like a bloated cow. It don't represent the county no more; it ain't first town any more. It's a has-been. Plaza is taking the records and Plaza is assuming the job. If they's any killings, it's your fault for being stubborn. And if they is any murder trials held, they'll take place in Plaza from now on. Figure it for yourself. What Plaza jury or judges is a-going to convict a Plaza man? Think it over."

But Sheriff Foshay's head swung from side to side in dissent. He stood as the target for forty-odd guns; he would be the first man to fall. Safety, life, everything desirable was to be had by stepping down. The rest of the men in Smoky River would obey his gesture, for it was his own stubborn spirit that kept them to fighting pitch, it was his sense of right that stirred their own pride. His tall, rangy figure cut an outline in the courthouse door, unwavering. He could not step down; he carried the badge that meant law. In his mind, which held only a few straightforward ideas, there wasn't even an argument. To step down meant betrayal of all order, a denial of everything his office stood for. So he shook his head.

"You can't bust up the courthouse, boys. I won't allow it. There is a right way to do this and a wrong way. You're going at it wrong. Go home and vote for Plaza next election, that's the right way." Then his words shot out, sharper, more commanding. "Is there any fellow in Plaza who can say I didn't give him a fair deal? You know better. You're a bunch of cat's-paws for a man who ain't even here to share the trouble. Go on back home."

"Get out of the way!" yelled Gilpin. "Or we'll plug you!"

"Go ahead," said Bill Foshay. "I'm standing right here. You don't want the county records that bad."

Joe Breedlove was shaking his head when the first gun explosion shook Smoky River from end to end, and a sense of physical sickness swept over him — the only time such a thing had happened to him since that dim, remote day when he had witnessed his first gun battle. A great man was passing on while he stood by, helpless. Sheriff Foshay's arms were spread out as if he were blocking the door; then the grave, rugged face tipped like that of a supremely weary man, and he buckled forward, sliding down the steps and rolling up to Nig Gilpin's horse.

A wild, desperate yell split the sluggish air and bedlam smashed and upset every impulse, every sober thought. Guns roared, the belch of powder and the flail of lead filling the cramped space. Horses reared; Joe saw Indigo's face turned in mute appeal to him, drawn and infuriated; but he kept shaking his head. Nig Gilpin was emptying his gun like a crazy man, weaving from side to side. Saddles were empty, the group on the courthouse steps had dissolved before the fury of the Plaza men's attack; glass fell in sprays from the second-story windows, and a man went staggering into the saloon, both hands folded over his stomach.

A woman's scream sheered through the more brutal echoes; Sheriff Foshay's daughter ran out of the hotel, ducked around Joe's restraining arm and plunged into the fury where her father lay. Up from the rear of town raced a magnificent chestnut horse. The dust rose. Slash LeGore sat above it, straight and imperturbable, calling out to his men in a pitch that seemed hardly more than casual. Yet they heard; the firing slackened and his flat monotone carried even to the second-story windows.

"That's enough, boys. Blood's been let. Killing ain't any good. Hold your fire, Gilpin. You done wrong. You started this play to satisfy a personal grudge and you'll have a talk with me about that. Smoky River, stop the shooting. We can wipe out this town if we choose, but we ain't disposed to carry on any hog-sticking contest. Stop the shooting. Back away from those windows, you. Get clear of the courthouse. We aim to take the records away. Anybody want to die for a few lousy sheets of paper?"

Foshay was gone and with him went the stiffening that had carried Smoky River to this point of resistance. There wasn't a voice raised, excepting that of the red-headed youth who slouched against the wall with blood dripping down his fingers and cursing Gilpin with a full heart. LeGore flipped his wrist.

"All right. Get inside. Few of you catch up some wagons from yonder stable. Work fast."

The Plaza men split to perform the varied chores. Slash LeGore dipped his head a moment at the dead sheriff and seemed to muse, making a fair target of himself for any rebellious or discontented Smoky River man. A nerveless creature; sinister and powerful. He swung in to the porch and confronted the partners with a glimmer of recognition in his shuttered eyes.

"Stayed out of the fight, I see."

Joe nodded, impassive and curt.

"Had you figured different," went on Slash LeGore. "I seldom mistake a man. What held you back?"

"Personal reasons."

"See you didn't take my hint. Bought out Bonnick anyhow."

"You appear to know what's going on," said Joe, blue eyes chilling.

"I do. Always do. The name of LeGore means something around here. Ask and find out. You're wise in not fighting, but you're foolish not to clear the country like I meant you to do when I warned Bonnick. Get out and stay out."

"You go to hell!" snapped Indigo. "I got a notion to — "

Slash LeGore ignored the small partner completely, interrupting the angry retort. "I choose the sort of people I want to stay around here. You ain't the kind I want for neighbors. Might cause me trouble. So travel."

"We'll stick," said Joe, even and flat.

"I judge," replied LeGore, equally toneless. He let a silence fall while he tipped his head forward and considered the man before him, The wagons were up and Plaza men were systematically gutting the courthouse. Record books, files, instruments, desks, all these things came out in a steady stream to be piled into the vehicles. A group labored profanely down the steps with the safe. Gilpin was trying to catch LeGore's attention.

"You're the kind to make me trouble," droned LeGore. "I say for the last time, get out of the country and stay out. Next time I won't do no talking."

Joe's chest lifted. Anger stiffened his features and light flashed across his eyes. "That's what I've been waiting for. I said I'd make no untoward move. Your kind is poison to me. We always collide. But I was waiting for you to push in your chips first. We'll stick, LeGore. I have seen enough to sicken me this afternoon. We'll meet again, don't worry about that."

"I judge," grunted LeGore.

Gilpin came up and spoke a few words, his brutal face swollen with lust and destruction. LeGore, as gray and enigmatic as a slice of granite, stared at Gilpin until the latter flinched away. Joe, who knew a great deal about the human heart, dismissed Gilpin as so much trash, even though he looked the more evil of the twain. It was Slash LeGore who carried behind his nerveless countenance the ultimate degree of wanton, cold courage.

The splendid chestnut turned and carried the man out of Smoky River alone. Gilpin's rough oaths slashed at the crowd, the wagons moved on down the street and across the bridge. Dusk came to the ransacked town and a weary, desolate silence that was broken only by the sound of the girl, as she knelt in the dust beside her dead father and cried her youth away.

Chapter 3

In that stricken town where the blue tendrils of dusk softly settled down to enshroud the wreckage, men were slowly recoiling from the hot breath of death, wrapped in their own emotions. It was Joe Breedlove, whose heart was quick to feel the distress of others and whose kindly eyes saw what men didn't usually see, who stepped into the trampled dust of the street and bent beside the girl. He said nothing, for there was nothing to say; but he lifted her away with an overflowing gentleness and turned her toward the hotel, one bronzed hand patting her shoulder in the manner in which he would have comforted a child. She was blind to the steps and blind to the wide door, nor did she see the chair he led her to, a battered and ancient rocker that he pulled around as she sank down. Other men in their attempt to soothe, would only have hurt her the worse; Joe sat beside her and slowly swayed the rocker. It was just a little thing, but this silver-templed man knew the power little things had. Dim memory told him. That undulating movement would reach down to numb, in some small measure, the profound agony racking her.

And so it did. The brown-haired head fell forward on a rocker arm, pillowed by a clenched fist, while her crying ran free and unabated. Men came in. Joe shook his head and they went out on tiptoe. The proprietor struck a match to a lamp, but the quick signal told him to leave the place in semi-darkness. From time to time Joe dropped his lean fingers across her temples, thinking back to when his own mother had done this and he had forgotten his own childish misfortunes. Thinking back, as well, to his own brief hour of romance when another girl, white and stricken in the pale moonlight, had cried on his shoulder. In such a manner did the patterns of life repeat themselves in this transitory existence. Men were built to stand the swift tragedy of the world; it was different with women. Tonight this girl was placing something fine and fresh behind her, nor would it ever return.

The red-headed youth started in. Joe rose and pushed him back to the porch. "Not right this minute, son," he murmured. "Let her alone a little while. What could you be saying that would help?"

The youth choked. "I'm going to follow that gang as long as there's strength in my body! I am going to kill Gilpin. I am going to see the blood run out of him! That's what I'll tell her!"

"And every word of it would hit her like a hammer," was Joe's grave answer. "You can't say it tonight, boy. I reckon you love her. If you do, think about her a little more. Tonight you've got to take the place of her dad. You won't ever be able to do it, but you've got to try. Go in there after a bit and take her home. Say nothing about revenge till you've slept on it. Let the killing be done by those who've already been tainted by it. No matter how clear a case you've got, another man's life never makes a soft pillow at night. What's wrong with your arm?"

"Nothing," muttered the youth. "A little gun blaze on it. Don't talk to me about killing, mister! I emptied one saddle and I wish to God I'd emptied 'em all!"

"Sleep on it," repeated Joe very quietly. "And don't go in there with malice on your tongue. It is help she wants."

The youth caught hold of himself. "I know.

You talk like her dad. He always was fair. Thanks. I'll be going now."

He left. Joe stood on the porch watching the courthouse steps. A party had come up and taken the sheriff inside. Lanterns bobbed along, hovering over other still, cramped bodies in the dust. Four men had died in the brief compass of a dozen gun lashes. Indigo came out of the porch gloom and cleared his throat, cigarette tip cutting a jagged track in the darkness.

"You and me have been together a long time, Joe. I ain't ever reproached you when I was sober. Mebbe you got to live by your conscience. A man's go to do as he sees. I won't say nothing more about it, but I ain't ever going to feel right about standing back while the sheriff went buckling down. I don't think we done proper."

"Maybe," sighed Joe. "But it wasn't conscience, Joe. I was ready to pull and plow ahead when Gilpin opened the ball. But do you see those two middle windows on the second floor of the courthouse across the way — the ones directly in line with these steps?"

"Yeah."

"There was a gun muzzle pushed out from each window when the Plaza crowd moved in. You didn't see 'em. I did. One gun was lined up with your vest buttons. The other was spotted on my liver. They was waiting for us to make a bad move."

"Hell!" grunted Joe. "I thought — I guess I'm a dam' fool! But how could any of the Plaza bunch get up there so sudden?"

"They didn't. Some of the men in town was there waiting. Smoky River is rotten with deceit."

"If this bunch don't rise up and go back to smash Plaza — "

"No. These boys won't. When Foshay died the starch went out of Smoky River. They're scared, they're licked. If another man like the sheriff could whip 'em into shape, they might try, but no such man walks the street right now. Don't blame 'em for being scared by LeGore. I'm spooky of the creature myself."

"Don't talk thataway," protested Indigo. "It ain't right and it ain't seemly."

A rider came posting across the bridge and reined in before the loitering party by the courthouse. "Say," he called, "my wagons nearly ran over a dead man four miles down the road. Right where the river bends in. It's Henry Bonnick, shot through the roof of his skull. Where's the sheriff?"

Joe's arm rose and dropped in the shadows.

One of the Smoky River men spoke up

after a long silence. "Good God, did they get him, too? Say, Kearwill, this town is full of dead men. The Plaza bunch just hit us like a ton of dynamite and ran off with the county records."

"So! That finally happened, did it? I've felt that in the air a long time. Thought I heard firing from the road. I left a man to wait by Bonnick until somebody got there. We'd better get Foshay busy on it."

"Foshay," muttered the spokesman, "is riding down the trail with Bonnick. Foshay was killed."

"Foshay!"

"Bonnick will have to lay in the road tonight," went on the spokesman. "There ain't a stitch of authority left around here. It's a coroner's job and Doc Spears went out on a call this aft'noon. Won't be back till late."

Kearwill, the rider, was muttering something that was drowned out by a rising rumble and clank from the bridge. A long line of freight wagons rolled across the structure and halted in the street; ten or twelve great vehicles, mule drawn. White tarps gleamed over high, rounding loads. Water buckets jangled, harness gear clashed, while the profanities of the muleskinners sent a new spurt of life through Smoky River. The old teams were free of their loads and going into the stable. Fresh mules came out.

Joe's question stopped a passing townsman. "What's this outfit?"

"Freighters bound from the railroad to the mines in yonder hills. They change here, eat a four-o'clock breakfast in Plaza and reach the mines by sunup. You can set your watch by this outfit, mister."

Indigo was restless again. "Well, Joe?"

"Yeah. We take a hand in this. We start right from the spot they killed Bonnick. But we better wait for the coroner and ride out with him. Meanwhile, let's turn in and catch a wink. I want to sleep off some of what I saw today. Do you see the end of this, Indigo? The end is when LeGore and me stand apart and shoot it out. I don't know who killed Bonnick, and I don't know what all this means. But I do know the trail ends with LeGore and me."

In complete silence they strolled to the restaurant, had coffee and walked into the stable, rolling up in some loose straw. "When the Doc comes in," Joe told the roustabout, "you call us."

Indigo fell to snoring almost immediately, but Joe Breedlove, flat on his back, stared at the black vault above. His sensitive mind held every scene in clear and sharp outline: Bonnick spurring out of Smoky River, the tall and fine figure of Bill Foshay towering above the renegades and at last falling, his girl crying in the dust. A man with a lesser imagination could have put them aside; in Joe they kept burning deeper and deeper, rousing the powerful, sweeping anger. LeGore's gray face was before him and a chill, tight runner of emotion passed through the tall partner. Men who lived by the gun died by the gun. All his life he had tried to find the peace he desired and yet he was forever finding himself isolated in the white glare of violence. Someday he would go down. This might be the end of the trail for him; LeGore was the better man.

It was not yet daylight when the roustabout came growling back to their straw bed. Doc Spears' buggy was waiting in the street and the Doc himself was eating breakfast. The partners washed at the pump and hurried down to the restaurant to find Spears, a grizzled little man with drawn eyes, drinking coffee by lamplight. The redheaded youth was there also and another man that Joe found himself instinctively measuring. A laconic introduction revealed the fellow as a deputy by the name of Cash Cairns. There was nothing imposing about Cairns; he was all bone and skin, sorrel-complexioned and lack-lustre of eye. Merely grunting at the partners, he finished his meal and sauntered out. Spears took his absence as an opportunity to quiz the redhead.

"Where was Cairns during the shooting?"

"Out of town."

"He would be. Well, let's go."

The doctor and the youth rode in the buggy while the partners and Cairns followed behind. Once Spears motioned for Joe to come abreast and talked to him.

"Being strangers here, what's your interest in Bonnick?"

"We bought his place," explained Joe. "He was warned not to sell, but he took the chance and ran. That's why he was killed."

"Who warned him?" snapped the doctor.

Joe shook his head. "I don't pack stories, Doc. You judge for yourself. The first guess would be right."

Suddenly the doctor stiffened and struck his buggy side with a full blow of his hand. "I have seen too many men buried in the last five years! All trails lead to one man. I wish I were half as old. I'd take that trail!"

By the first faint flush of light they came to the bend of the river and stopped before a sprawled body in the road. The man left by Kearwill to watch, crawled out from behind a boulder, grumbling. "Thought nobody was never going to come. Next time somebody else can set in on the wake. Not me."

The doctor was down beside Bonnick. The redhead never left the buggy seat; after all that had happened the night before this scene made no impression on him. Neither did Cash Cairns dismount.

"Shot and stripped of his valuables," declared the doctor.

"He was carrying around four hundred dollars," said Joe. "We gave it to him."

"Plain case of robbery," put in Cairns. "Happens every day. The fool had ought to've known better."

The doctor looked up at Joe, lips compressing. He moved an arm and the partners lifted Bonnick into the back of the buggy and tucked a piece of canvas over him. The watcher crowded into the seat and Doc Spears turned about.

"We drop off here," announced Joe. "See you later."

The doctor understood. "Good luck," he muttered. "I'd like to be man enough to go along."

The redhead caught the meaning then and started to climb down. "Hold on," objected Joe. "You ain't got any horse and this is none of your business. You stick by Foshay's girl till we come back."

The rig went on. Cairns lingered just a

moment, seeming sullenly suspicious. "How'd I know you ain't in this Bonnick deal? Where you heading for?"

"You ain't big enough to ask questions," snorted Indigo. "Take a ride."

"Oh, I dunno about that!" grunted Cairns. He shifted in the saddle and studied the partners for a short period. Wheeling the horse, he threw a last warning over his shoulders. "I wouldn't get too damned curious. Cemeteries is crowded in this country."

Indigo held his peace until the deputy passed beyond earshot, then contented himself with a croaking observation. "You ain't a fit specimen for decent burial. You're buzzard bait."

Joe rode along the rutted trail, eyes fixed on the dust as the morning light strengthened. Presently he beckoned Indigo to come ahead.

"Funny hoof print there. Take a good look at it."

Indigo slid from the saddle and stooped until his sharp nose was almost on top of the track. "This hoss didn't have no shoes, Joe. Barefoot. Injun style. They ain't no Injuns around here."

"Let's keep following a ways."

The two of them quested along for the best part of a mile. At that point the trail of the barefoot pony curved sharply in from the desert. At this point, too, the marks of Bonnick's pony made a sudden circle from south to north and doubled back toward Smoky River.

"This killer," said Joe, "was out there behind some juniper, waiting. Bonnick is fogging along for the railroad when the killer moved out into sight. Bonnick sees him. Bonnick says his prayers, turns and makes a run for town. Maybe there is a little lead swapped but Bonnick is scared; it's his showdown and he knows it. The barefoot pony creeps up on him and when he gets to about the river's bend a bullet tears out his lights. The killer chased him a mile, Indigo. Now let's go see what happens to the barefoot pony next."

The intervening passage of the freighters had, of course, scuffed up the trail of pursued and pursuer, but they picked it up at the point where both had veered into the soft soil beside the road. Once more by the spot where Bonnick had fallen the partners began cutting circles into the desert; and it was Indigo who first crossed the barefoot pony's spoor as it led away from the point of the murder. Arrow-straight and apparently without attempt at subterfuge or concealment, it led east toward the hills.

"Toward Plaza San Felipe," murmured Joe.

"Well?"

"We follow, Indigo. We find that pony and the man that rode him."

"LeGore? He wasn't a riding no such unshod brute when he hit Smoky River."

"Maybe not. Somebody else might have killed Bonnick. Did you observe that Gilpin got out of our sight when Bonnick cleared town yesterday afternoon? Him or LeGore, or maybe somebody else again. Don't matter. This trail leads to LeGore in the end. Let's go."

They kept to the trail, and after a half mile forded the Smoky at a shallowing gravel bar. The sun glared over the rim, full against them and the dust began to rise, against which even the lifted bandanna was ineffectual. They fell into arroyos and rose again to the sweeping, level plain. The outline of Smoky River town shifted from left flank to rear. Still the trail of the barefoot pony, cut deep from fast travel, kept its direct line. But after something like three quarters of an hour the partners arrived at a point where the tracks broke away from a compass course and described a semicircle. Presently they reached a road, a furrowed yellow trace stretching between rival towns; upon this were the marks of all last night's travel, of raiders and freight teams alike, and lost somewhere in the scuff of so many horses was the trail of the barefoot pony.

Indigo looked back toward Smoky River. Joe shook his head, and they pressed on eastward until many hoofs overflowed the narrow ribbon of road into the softer sand.

"That killer met the Plaza bunch here yesterday afternoon," announced Joe. "And prob'ly joined them to come back and make the attack."

"In which case," countered Indigo, "that unshod pony is in or around Plaza now. But if said horse was in the gang last night, how was it we didn't see it?"

"You and me weren't looking at much of anything except LeGore and Gilpin."

"Neither of which rode any barefoot pony. Does that take them two buzzards out of the picture? Mebbe, mebbe not. Anyhow, Plaza is the town we want to give a look and it ain't going to be fun. Nobody is going to give us any keys to the city, Joe."

They went on, lagging in the brassy atmosphere. Smoky River's outline dimmed behind them; that of Plaza San Felipe appeared as a charcoal mark drawn across the base of a tawny butte. Joe studied it, lids dropped well over his eyes.

"Won't help our prospects none to be spotted from that town by a pair of glasses. They'll be keeping a watch on this road. Let's cut a circle to the north and get around to the base of them hills. They ain't going to bother much about Plaza's back door."

"Uh-uh," grunted Indigo and turned off the road. Increasing the distance by two hours' ride or more meant nothing to the partners when they had a good half day to kill; it would be impossible to enter Plaza by daylight. Thus they cut their circle, utilizing every arroyo to keep below the plane of visibility. At noon they stopped for rest beneath a juniper. South of them a dust stringer marked the passage of a hurried rider, posting toward Plaza. Without a word the partners amplified the circle and around six o'clock found themselves crawling the base of the bench land after an infinitely hot and tedious trip. A mile or more ahead was a butte slightly separated from the main line of hills; and behind the butte lay Plaza. The sun, blurring the western line with its blood red fury, still had a half hour to set; the partners threw themselves in a small pocket and tarried.

All the day Joe had been extraordinarily silent and moody and restless. He was in a frame of mind in which Indigo had never before seen him, though they had traveled together for better than two years. He seemed plunged in harsh, unpleasant thoughts, his face was tightly drawn, nor had he displayed at any time since the previous night's affray that relaxing smile which had carried him through so many taut situations. As the last fragment of sun dropped below the horizon with a shower of sullen rays he turned soberly to Indigo.

"Any doubt in your mind about this party of ours?"

"What the hell's the matter with you?" snapped Indigo.

"This wouldn't happen in a thousand years," mused Joe, watching the shadows creep up along the bench. "We're walking into another man's town and another man's game. We're looking for a pony in a town full of ponies. Any other time and any other place we'd be minding our own business. This is dubious, Indigo. Damned ticklish. We ain't seen the beginning or the end yet. But it's LeGore. You and me can't expect to live in this country until we meet LeGore and settle the argument. That's the only reason we're bucking something even fools wouldn't buck. That's all I've got to say."

"Shadows coming," was Indigo's laconic statement. "Let's amble. Any particular plan of action in your bonnet?"

“No. We take what comes and work from that.”

The butte was slowly being absorbed in the cobalt shades. Joe and Indigo pressed on, left the flat country behind and zigzagged up the considerable slope. When they reached the summit and found themselves on a tablelike area it was dark and a faint glow rose from the depths beyond. Leaving their horses, they walked forward a hundred yards and arrived at the rim of a clifflike wall. It was not a sheer drop but it ran four hundred feet down with less than a hundred feet of horizontal slope. At the bottom lay Plaza San Felipe aglimmer with lights. Indigo, falling back on shrewd experience, began to take stock of the place. The places most brilliantly illuminated were, naturally, saloons. There were seven of these strung along the main street facing the butte, which seemed but a continuation of the road passing from Smoky Hill to the mountains. Behind this street lay a darker one and behind that again lay a row of dark ’dobe huts — Mexican quarters. Alleys, pitch-black, connected the three rows of tenements.

“They’re on the watch,” murmured Joe. “I can make out guards posted beyond town.”

“A mean looking joint,” grunted the small

partner. "We got to cross that main street and get down them alleys. Can't make out any stables from here. But there'd ought to be two-three in a place run by rustlers and mine operators."

"First off we rummage around and see what the place is like," said Joe. "It is just slightly possible that pony may be nosed in to some hitching rack. Or it may be in a stable. Or it may not even be in town. Then we watch for Gilpin and LeGore. If we get either of those gents in the right spot, we take 'em back to Smoky River."

"Providing they'll come," said Indigo.

"It never pays to plan too far ahead," replied Joe. "We've always had better luck just boosting in and waiting for something to break. Let's go."

They ranged the rim until they found the mouth of a trail. Down it they crawled, boots heels digging in to check the sharp pull of gravity. Presently they crouched at the bottom, behind a ramshackle shed, and peered around it. Forty feet across the way was a hotel's porch on which men loitered and smoked. Joe muttered a brief word to Indigo and flanked the street until they were deep in a clutter of corrals. The town's glow stopped short of this area and so in comparative security they rose up and started to circle around toward the other side of Plaza.

Something moved in the darkness. Both partners fell flat in the dust. An obscure rider came from the direction of the hills into the mouth of the street and halted. He seemed to have heard the partners or to suspect the area of the corrals on general principle. Shifting, he issued a slow, "*Quién es?*"

Indigo's arm wiggled downward toward his belt. The rider veered the horse and cut toward the corrals, passing the prone partners a yard away. The trample of his horse's hoofs diminished; Joe and Indigo rose in unison, strode rapidly across the street end and reached the blank side of some deserted building. Continuing on, they came to the second street. There was a saloon in the middle of it, which Joe judged to be a Mexican joint from its frowsy cramped appearance. But there were fewer lights in this quarter and many less pedestrians.

"A lot of miners roaming around loose tonight," murmured Joe. "I think we can keep ambling along without notice if we keep shaded. They've got a strong guard posted around this rustlers' roost, but as long as we didn't create any ruckus getting in we can move easier."

"Yeah, but we don't look like miners. Hope to thunder we never will."

They passed along the walk. What appeared to be the rear door of a block-long stable yawned beside them, all dark save for a single lantern up front. Dull glows came out of smudged shop windows adjoining, hardly strong enough to betray them. Soft Spanish drifted through doors; men passed, a pair of riders idled down and abreast of the partners, then vanished in an alley.

When Joe and Indigo reached the alley it was clear, the dark recesses of it seeming to invite them. By common consent they followed it back to Plaza San Felipe's main thoroughfare and stood beside a breast-high porch. It was dark here and the sidewalk jogged around it, diverting the wandering citizens. Joe and Indigo climbed up and sat on a bench.

But Indigo was getting restless, and when in that frame of mind he began to cook up ideas.

"We'll be here till daylight if we go at it this rate. Let's split. You take one half of the town, I'll tackle the other. We'll see what we see and meet again back yonder where we first crossed over. Those fellows have got to be around here some place, but we got to keep traveling to spot 'em."

"You know what happened last time we split," objected Joe.

"What of it? We got to be brisk about this. We won't try to brace anybody, we'll just get lined up and meet to talk it over."

"All right. At that street corner in a half hour."

"Yeah," grunted Indigo. He dropped off the porch and vanished.

Joe, instantly regretting the decision, adopted a bolder procedure. Pulling his sombrero lower on his head he joined in the trickle of pedestrians and sauntered eastward, studying the racked horses along the route. Whenever he found himself in front of too revealing a beam of light he dipped his head slightly and pressed across it. In this manner he passed a pair of saloons, the front end of the stable and arrived at a restaurant, suddenly conscious of hunger and thirst. Turning, he went back to the stable and tarried a little behind the beams of the lantern. Near the lantern and the four or five men swapping lies on the adjoining bales stood a water bucket and dipper. Joe ambled in without comment and helped himself to a drink. Nobody paid him particular notice; the drawling speech went on evenly until a brisk little whippet of a man strode in for his horse. The lantern went hobbing down the stable, flashing from stall to stall. Joe's eyes followed and found nothing of interest. Quite casually he walked out and on westward toward what appeared to be the center of the town's convivial spirit.

If LeGore were in Plaza, he probably would be in some private office, for the man was too harsh a character to spend a great deal of his time in front of a bar. But Joe was morally certain that Gilpin would be nowhere else than in a saloon; that was Gilpin's type. So as the tall partner approached the saloons he loitered by the open doors and casually glanced in; neither the first nor the second gave him any information. This exhausted his territory. The other saloons were in the section Indigo had taken, yet Joe, feeling that he was not pressing his luck far enough, started on. He passed the alley's mouth and walked leisurely toward the fanwise glow coming from the largest saloon in town. Just before venturing into all this brightness he checked his pace out of caution and swept the faces of the men idling around him.

At that moment a shot broke from the rear of Plaza San Felipe, followed by a second.

A pair of horsemen, possibly the same that had ridden by the partners on the other street, swerved and galloped into the alley.

A handful of men broke out of odd corners, like sentries answering a call, and hurried after, warning Joe that the town was more closely watched than he had come to believe. The saloon doors were opened to emit a party of men, and the tall partner, throwing himself back against a building wall, saw the unmistakable face of Cash Cairns bearing toward him. The deputy from Smoky River was even looking at the very spot Joe stood but the bright light of the saloon from which he had just come blurred his eyes. Another moment and he would have come into collision with Joe, but there was a clatter of many ponies entering Plaza from the hills and Cash Cairns stopped abruptly and turned to look. Slash LeGore, stiff and taciturn, rode by on the star-chested horse, reining before a building directly beyond the big saloon. Cairns called to the renegade chief and shouldered impatiently toward the man.

The disturbance out back grew more pronounced. Other men, sensing trouble, were sucked down the dark alley. Joe's muscles stiffened. He had a premonition that Indigo was in difficulties. Swinging wide away from the saloon lights, he jumped into the alley.

Chapter 4

LeGore walked into the marshal's office of Plaza San Felipe, followed by a dozen or so of his henchmen. The marshal sat before his desk, but on the appearance of LeGore he rose awkwardly and stepped back. The renegade chief strode about the place, his gray face set like granite and a quirt dangling from his wrist. Now and then along the route of his restless pacing he lifted the quirt to slash the walls and the piles of records that had been stored here after the attack on Smoky River.

"Where's Gilpin?"

The marshal shook his head. "I dunno. Last I saw he was over at the Blue Bucket."

That brought out a cold anger. "I'll ram a bottle down his throat some day and he'll drink no more. What's that shooting about?"

"Just another personal argument, I reckon,"

said the marshal. "Town's full up tonight."

Cash Cairns pushed his way through the group. "I been waiting all afternoon to tell you something, Slash — "

"You'll wait longer if I say so," droned LeGore, "and like it."

"Sure, sure," muttered Cairns. "I ain't growling about it, am I? But them two strangers which bought out Bonnick started thisaway early in the morning."

"Am I supposed to get worried?" snapped LeGore. Nevertheless a heavy silence fell over the place; a single furrow cut into his forehead. He swung on the marshal. "What the hell you doing in here with that ruckus going on outside? It might be those two fools. If it is, I want 'em brought to me."

"I slung a circle of men around this town," countered the marshal. "They ain't able to get in. An angleworm couldn't get in Plaza tonight."

"Neither you nor anybody else in Plaza is slick enough to keep them jaspers out if they got a mind to come in," retorted LeGore. "They're old heads and a match for all you clubfoot dumbwits put together. Now get out there and see what's wrong."

The marshal left. LeGore studied his other followers, a frigid and ironic gleam playing in the eye slits. An almost imperceptible move of his hand sent them shuffling back to the street, all but a pair of hulking, malevolent creatures who lounged tight-lipped against the wall — LeGore's lieutenants. In the long, grim silence following, LeGore paced around and around the table.

"I didn't want Bill Foshay killed," he finally announced. "He's the one man in the country who had a following. They might get together and cause us trouble. That's the hell of it — you give a man like Gilpin orders and he goes nutty trying to carry 'em out. I'll shoot the lights from that drunk, fatheaded digger one of these days."

He never lifted his voice on a single word, yet there was a venom, a deadliness in the flat monotone. The lieutenants stood rooted and silent.

"But since Foshay's knocked over, I'm changing my plans. Stretching out into better country. These hills around here are too crowded with mines, too far away from the big cattle outfits. We're going up into the canyons of the Smoky."

"By Bonnick's?" murmured one of the lieutenants.

"That's right."

"How about Craw Magoon and his men? They always considered the upper Smoky as private stamping ground."

"That yellow-dog," droned LeGore and brushed the subject aside. "We change headquarters tonight. We pass by way of Foshay's ranch and haze off every hand left there. If there's any argument, we make a bonfire and burn every stick of wood to the ground. In the following week we drive every brute wearing a Foshay brand up the Smoky. Bonnick's place is our headquarters."

"How about the girl — Foshay's girl, Chief?"

LeGore's gray face never changed; he didn't answer. The more curious of the spokesmen let it ride and changed the line of questioning.

"This is your town now, Chief. You got it in the hollow of your hand. Why move away?"

"It's my county now," said LeGore. "I pull the ring wherever I go. I'm stretching out. Go get the boys together."

The marshal stumbled over his own door sill, breathing hard. "Say, Chief, a little bit of a dried up runt near killed Gilpin! One of the boys say it's a stranger that rode into Smoky River with another guy — a tall pilgrim. The little feller's got away, but he's around somewhere!"

LeGore stiffened. A cheerless smile struck the marshal. "So them partners wiggled into

Plaza after you said an angleworm couldn't get through? Those men are tougher than anybody I've got around here." The drone rose to a brittle, whiplike command. "Now get out of here and bring them two in! Both of 'em! You cover every crack and hole in Plaza. Come back here without 'em, and I'll take hide from your neck. Go on, the whole bunch of you!"

When they were gone he stood by the desk and looked through the open door. "I made a mistake," he muttered. "Knew they'd cause me trouble when I laid eyes on 'em first time. Should've took 'em when I had the chance. That big man reminded me of Foshay, but Foshay couldn't hold a candle to him. I played the cards wrong."

LeGore was a supreme egoist, without a scruple, without a conscience. He lusted after power and there was in him a cruel Asiatic strain that exulted in seeing other men buckle beneath him or physically suffer. To admit the power of another man, as he did now, only served to inflame him. So, slashing the desk with his quirt, he strode out of the office, knocking aside some passerby who came unconsciously across his path. The main street was almost emptied of townsmen. Back of the town the full voice of the pack was lifted and an occasional shot exploded into the dark sky.

In the first place, Indigo had suggested the division of forces to Joe because he nurtured in the back of his little pea-shell head some immature plan of taking the town apart personally and immediately in order to find LeGore and Gilpin — and the barefoot pony.

Under the stress of danger Indigo had the attacking instinct of a king cobra; he didn't know the meaning of fear and, what was sometimes regrettable, he had less than a nodding acquaintance with caution. When thoroughly roused the dynamic fighting instinct of the man drove him ahead until something happened or somebody fell. He knew well enough that as long as he remained with Joe nothing like that would happen. Joe's method was different; Joe would remain in the shadows, waiting for the break of fortune with all the cast-iron patience of an Indian. Therefore, Indigo vanished within the obscurity of the Plaza and San Felipe's back section.

The red star of his fortune glimmered down on his umbrella stetson almost immediately. He had skimmed the alley as far as the second and less illuminated street and was about to plunge on toward the Mexican quarter when the side door of some dismal honkytonk was kicked wide open and three men passed through the yellow fan of light. Indigo drew back as if stung by a centipede, for the center fellow of the trio, issuing some thick and malicious profanity, wore a familiar face. That blunt, broken-nosed visage belonged to Gilpin, Sheriff Foshay's killer.

Indigo's immediate reaction was to dust off the butt of his gun with nervous fingers. The other two men, however, seemed stone sober and robust of constitution, so Indigo forebore. After a murmured argument all three ambled farther into the alley's mystery, left it and halted again beside a 'dobe hut with a high window pierced by a single fluttering ray of lamp glow. There was some more argument; then two of the party went away, leaving a third to fumble at the door latch of the hut. Indigo wasn't sure just who this third party was until the door opened and the light revealed Gilpin's brutal features. The man swayed on the threshold and called a name. There was no answer. Muttering irritably Gilpin went inside and started to close the door.

He never got it shut. Indigo's wasplike body ducked through the narrowing aperture in such a manner that he was carried almost to the center of the cramped room, stepping back as if he were walking on a floor of eggs, gun muzzle staring at Gilpin, who for one long moment looked stupidly along the barrel.

"High like a house!" snapped Indigo. "I ain't got much time to waste and I sure ain't wasting none on you! Pull up them paws or I'll blow most of you back through that door!"

If Gilpin had entered the 'dobe drunk, he was stark sober thirty seconds thereafter. A purple glow darkened the whisky flush on his jowls; a sudden sweat film glistened on the blackened forehead. But his chest muscles spread against the tight surface of his vest as he obeyed the command. Whatever his feelings, he knew better than to disregard this bantam who looked as if he meant to fire anyhow. Neither grace nor charity had any part in that fighting mask with its shrewish slashes of skin and flickering jade orbs. Gilpin's hands went high. Still not grasping the import of this business, he ventured a husky growl.

"Who the hell are you? I ain't in the wrong shack, am I?"

"Reach over with your left hand, lift that gun with two fingers and let 'er drop," said Indigo.

"Seem to know your business, don't you? Sounds downright professional to me." The gun struck the floor and about the same time Gilpin's vision cleared. So did his memory. He swayed, his elbows buckled, he bellowed like a stabbed bull. "Why, you skinny little pilgrim! How'd you get in this town? Damn it, I'll fry the soles of your feet in the blacksmith forge so you won't move around so dam' easy! Now you git humble in a hurry! You saw what I did yesterday! I can do it again!"

"Uh-huh," grunted Indigo. "That's why I'm right here looking at you. You're going back to Smoky River where the rafters grow high and there's plenty of barrels to stand on. I'm a man that minds my own business, strictly, but you're just the kind of a cheap-john pig sticker which makes me wish I could treat you Indian style."

All this while he was stepping catlike around the room, for he had discovered the hut to have two rooms, separated by a gaudy red curtain. Now he stood commanding both Gilpin and the curtain. Gilpin rolled his swollen eyes at the curtain and then dropped them to the gun on the floor. The curtain parted and a buxom Mexican woman looked on the scene with sleepy eyes.

"Now lady," muttered Indigo, somewhat disconcerted, "you go on back. Gilpin, don't you try to make a dive for her. Walk away from that door. I'm going through it first and you're following me."

The woman laughed at Gilpin and murmured a soft Spanish phrase at him; but when the man answered back, short and imperative, the laughter changed to a flame of anger that beat against the small partner. Indigo understood no Spanish, but he had a good idea of what she was saying and a better idea of what she meant to do. She was coming forward, this bronzed and husky Delilah, with her arms akimbo, sidling slowly around to put herself between the gun and Gilpin.

Indigo, who had absolutely no mode of defense against a female, backed away to keep his drop on the renegade. "You start something," he warned Gilpin, "behind her petticoats and you won't have no further need of yourself." Then he swung on the woman again, irritable and nervous. "Now lady, it ain't a woman's part to dabble in this kind of a mess. It just ain't seemly."

She kept sidling forward, dusky eyes flashing. Indigo, who was hardy enough to walk into a lion pit and give the lion first swipe, fidgeted this way and that, a feeling of helpless desperation coming over him. He didn't know whether the lady meant to hug him or scratch him.

"Call off this female wrassler!" he warned Gilpin.

Gilpin snapped a harsh word at her. She screamed, which further demoralized the hectored Indigo, lifted her arms and came clawing at him. Indigo yelled, "Now, lady, no woman had ought to do such things!" and tried to break her attack. Her nails slashed his face and the pressure of her ample body drove the little man against the wall so hard that he bit himself. She slapped him so hard his ears rang; she hauled him away from the wall and fought for the gun he vainly tried to hold on Gilpin.

Afoul all this calico Indigo saw Gilpin dive forward and with a mighty surge he threw the woman way from him and fired point blank. The bullet smashed plaster, missing Gilpin by a foot. Then the renegade and the woman struck him from both sides at once, flattened him between them, and knocked him to the floor; the lady, seeming to posses some diabolic knowledge of Indigo's weak spot, screamed again, this time right in his ear. Gilpin's fist landed on the point of his peaked nose and Gilpin's bulky body punched the air out of him

With his back to the floor, Indigo tapped that reserve of fury that in a crisis like this made of him a fighting wildcat. He became a boneless, squirming dervish. Gilpin's fists lost their target and broke against the clay floor; moreover, the lady in her attempt to do damage to the intruder, lost her sense of direction and sank her claws into Gilpin. This resulted in the renegade's slacking his effort on Indigo to knock her away.

The lady, now extremely impartial in her anger, scratched Gilpin again and tried to twist his ear. Indigo rolled aside and made a headlong dive for his gun which had been knocked out of his fist. The lady executed a swift turn from Gilpin and caught one of Indigo's boots, pulling it off. Gilpin sprang after Indigo, was shunted aside by Indigo's rearing feet, and went sprawling into the corner. Indigo fired again and missed again. The lady rushed him, but Indigo, in mortal terror of having her yell in his ear, made two complete somersaults and fell out of the 'dobe hut, landing on his feet. He never stopped moving. Twenty yards into the darkness he heard Gilpin bawling for Plaza San Felipe to crowd in and head off the stranger among them; and in absolute defiance to all laws of safety Gilpin fired four shots down the black street.

It seemed both impossible and unseemly to Indigo that this deserted section of town should sprout so many pursuing figures out of nowhere at all. Mexicans, punchers and miners flung themselves from houses and alleys to take up the chase and the cry in three different languages, all profane. He plunged into one such fellow at the mouth of the alley, hitting the man hard enough to break bone, and galloped on. At the moment it was entirely immaterial to Indigo where he headed; the main idea was to get away from there as fast as he could. So he fled through the alley, one boot off and one boot on, came to the second street and kept right on going toward the most illuminated part of Plaza.

Almost immediately he discovered this to be a tactical error. The population of Plaza was thundering back from saloon, stable and restaurant; they came down the alleys, out of back doors, off second-story porches. None of them knew which way to go, but as they started toward the Mexican quarter the tidal wave rolled back from that area, turned them about and boosted them on.

Indigo meanwhile had wheeled away from the alley and was limping westward, hugging the blackest corners he could. He meant to break out of Plaza, circle the place and enter it again from the angle he and Joe had originally used. Back of him, the crowd had gotten tangled up by its own awkward proportions and was going around and around. Indigo saw safety to the fore and adopted more caution; but at the precise moment he crossed another of the town's connecting alleys he heard a lesser party of men swing down from the western end of this street and advance against him.

Thus boxed, Indigo lifted his eyes to last resources and saw an outside stairway climbing the side of a building. He took it three steps at a time, attained a landing and confronted a door that gave to tentative pressure. What was inside he didn't know, for an impenetrable pall filled it. But whatever it was, it was preferable to his exposed position; he left the landing and closed the door behind him.

He discovered nothing in the first few minutes except the outrageous condition of his own carcass. He was breathing like some steam-charged locomotive; his fists hurt, his scratched face stung him, he had soft and pulsing spots on every odd square inch of his frame; one of his good back teeth seemed a little slack on its moorings and his bootless foot was undoubtedly filled with splinters, nails and chewing tobacco labels.

By the time he had gotten command of his wind he felt like a lily wilted on the stem. During the same interval his senses adjusted themselves to the pitch dark interior and he began to hear sounds of men below him and to see faint pencils of light shooting up through minute cracks. Stepping to right and then to left his hands touched descending rafters. Ahead was the seeming source of the sounds that came to him; and since it was probable that sooner or later some misguided genius in the mob on the street would decide the stairway was worth inspecting it behooved him to look around for an alternate method of leaving this sultry, dead-air attic. Therefore, he went groping ahead. The pencils of light grew more pronounced and he thought he heard glass and chips clinking. Discovering a larger shaft of light coming up through the flooring, he decided to go over and lay an eye against it; a feeling of reassurance took hold of him and he stepped on — and met disaster.

The solid floor ended. His advancing foot pressed against some flimsy composition stuff that had been scantily tacked to the rafters from the under side to make a ceiling. At first pressure it gave way, and Indigo, fighting like a cat about to be thrown off a bridge, plunged between joists and fifteen feet down into the glare of a saloon. He thought he heard a great deal of glass come clattering after him, but at that moment he wasn't positive because he passed peacefully out of the scene.

When his senses straggled back to their frail tenement, Indigo discovered himself propped up between a pair of burly individuals and ranged around by a silent, fascinated crowd. He counted the business ends of three different guns gaping at him. The gray, dead face of LeGore hovered over him.

"I wonder," groaned Indigo, "what happened to my wings?"

Joe had gone through the alley shoulder to shoulder with several other men and was shunted aside in the town's second street by the rapidity of their passage. By that time the crowd had completely messed up whatever scent or trail the original pursuers had. Joe could see no single face clearly, but he distinguished one voice bellowing above the multitude and it seemed to him he had heard it before. But from the talk going on he had his fears confirmed — it was Indigo who had started the riot. Once more the little partner's genius for developing grief had achieved success. Joe, worried and apprehensive, could not suppress a grim hope that Indigo was satisfied with the net result.

Lanterns were bobbing through the crowd; some kind of self-inspection was in progress.

Several horsemen pushed westward and a sudden yell set the whole pack in motion. Joe, realizing the futility of trying to tag along, turned the other way. Indigo was probably clear of this fracas and on his way back to the rendezvous. So Joe traveled toward the rendezvous with circumspection and due deliberation, arrived there, and found no partner.

"Damn that ornery little buzzard of disaster! Someday he's going to sprain his neck from poking it into unnecessary grief."

A freshening hallo bearing along the street announced to Joe some new development. Thoroughly roused, he left the rendezvous and started back, seeing the crowd rounding the alley and headed for the main thoroughfare. Abreast of the stable's rear entrance he stopped to look down the block-long passageway. There was a solitary individual hitching a team to a flat-bed wagon; the other loiterers were out with the pack.

Joe lifted his shoulders and walked into the stable, casually skirted the busy teamster and stood within a dark angle of the front door. Men were swarming around the main saloon and a group of horses were lined against the walk. As he watched, unable to see anything in particular, a sizable party came from the saloon, took to saddle and turned east on the street, pushing the citizenry aside. At this point the teamster finished hitching and walked out. Joe's attention, momentarily diverted to this extraordinarily indifferent character, saw him enter the restaurant. Then the cavalcade advanced abreast the stable, and Joe's watching eyes hardened to the scene in front of him.

Indigo was a prisoner, feet tied under a pony's belly; beside him rode Slash LeGore on a wall-eyed, chunky little claybank. The lights of the restaurant played an instant on the party and at that point Joe discovered the claybank to be unshod. There was his barefoot pony. The cavalcade passed outward toward the hills.

Joe's rangy body sprang back into the stable. He took up the water bucket, half-filled, and pushed it along the bed of the waiting wagon. He ripped a saddle and bridle off a peg above the lantern and raced toward the stalls. Into the nearest one he ducked, slapped the saddle on a brute he couldn't see and hauled at the cinch so swiftly and savagely that the animal grunted and swayed against him. There was a group out on the walk, blocking the stable mouth as they argued about something. Joe paused only a moment; his Indian patience was gone and in its place was a crystal hard recklessness. He backed the horse away from the stall and led it rearward. There in the deeper shadows he adjusted the bridle, swung up and waited.

The teamster ambled back with what appeared to be a lunch basket, crawled to the seat and clucked his tongue. The arguing group split apart to allow the wagon's departure; it turned east on the street and rumbled away. Joe tarried a little longer and then rode through the back door to the town's darker thoroughfare and trotted also eastward. He rounded the building corner where he was to have met Indigo, angled to strike the main road into the hills and found the wagon and team clacking along some yards ahead of him. He checked speed, wanting the outfit to get farther away from Plaza before he overtook it. At that moment a horseman eased quietly into the road from some black pool by the corrals, blocking Joe's departure. A slow, level challenge reached him.

"Who're you, brother?"

Joe froze in the saddle. Yet the cool impulse of his long training in self-control put a lazy drawl in his voice as he answered, "Don't stop me now, Pete. Where's Slash gone? He walked out with me holding the sack."

"I ain't Pete, I'm Lem. Slash is just ahead of you. Take the left fork around the butte.

He's heading back towards Smoky River. Is this Mex Trimble?"

"A-huh. Hell of a time for Slash to be on the prod. I ain't had any sleep for a coon's age. Now I got to fog or he'll leave me miles behind." He touched his spurs and moved around. But the other man moved as well. Suspicion still lingered in his voice.

"I'm outa matches. You got one?"

"Sure," agreed Joe and reached into his vest pocket. But as the match came out his thumbnail clipped off the igniting tip. He passed it over and waited while the other man scratched it on the saddle horn

"No good," said the fellow. "Gimme another."

"What you trying to do," challenged Joe, dryly sarcastic, "get me in trouble with the chief? What you hanging around here for?"

"Orders. There's another jasper Slash wants which is around town somewhere. A big guy with a little silver in his mane. Teams up with that skinny runt we just took. Where's the match?"

"Shucks I ain't got any more. Back away. I can't stay here all night. If you can't light the matches folks give you, it'd be a good idea for you to carry a candle. So long." And Joe forced his way by, galloping past a muttered order to wait. He expected to be overhauled and headed in; but the sentry let him go. That wagon had gone on a few hundred yards and the driver had lighted a lantern and hung it to the brake handle. Joe galloped by, seeing a dark, taciturn face look up to him in passing. A quarter mile farther on the tall partner reined in and waited.

The teamster had settled his horses into a trotting pace and his piping voice rose in an unmelodious song. Joe lifted his gun and curled around a head high boulder. When the wagon was within ten yards he shot forward. "Just a minute, brother. Pull in."

The teamster's baked jaws tightened. He hauled on the reins and spat over the footboards. "Hell," he grunted, "you ain't a very bright road agent. What you expect to carry off me?"

"That lunch, friend. I need it worse than you. Hand it up."

The teamster complied, muttering his disgust at such proceedings. "Why didn't you fill your belly in town like a white man? Now I got to travel lean all night. When warts like you turn to penny ante larceny, it's high time for a house cleaning. Now what?"

"A bucket of water under your seat."

"I ain't got no bucket of water."

"Reach and feel for it."

The teamster swore when his exploring hand touched the bucket. "How'd that get here?"

"I put it there in the stable," said Joe. "Thanks for the service."

"Sa-ay," exclaimed the teamster, "you ain't one of them — "

"You ain't curious are you?" drawled Joe.

The teamster's teeth clicked down on the unfinished phrase. "No," he grunted. "I ain't a bit curious."

"Travel!"

Harness chains jingled in the crisp night, the wagon wheels chattered through the road ruts, and the lantern, diminishing in the distance, made a shimmering, yellow shield. Joe turned and cut around the base of the butte with half a bucket of water and a lunch pail. Twenty minutes later he arrived at the top of the butte, portioned the water between the long waiting ponies and ate the borrowed supper. Presently he rolled a cigarette, struck a match and cupped it between his hands. His gray eyes, narrowed down to thin apertures, flashed and the lean cheeks were as fixed and impassive as so much flint.

"Only reason LeGore towed Indigo along with him," he mused, "was to make bait for me. He knows Indigo and me is partners. He knows I'll follow to get Indigo out of the jackpot. So he aims to suck me into a trap."

He rose to the borrowed pony and descended the slope, leading the other two horses. Westward along the shadowed earth lay Smoky River. He aimed toward that ill-fortuned town, measuring his direction by the north star shining dimly above. Far out from the butte he spoke again.

"Well, he's got his chance. I'm following into a showdown. Him or me."

Chapter 5

Traveling through the grateful coolness of the night at a brisk gallop, Joe pondered over the problem of Slash LeGore. The renegade chief had killed Henry Bonnick. The fact that he was now riding the barefoot pony indicated as much, for a man of his authority would not share horses with anybody else — that is to say, no other would have ridden the pony at the time of Bonnick's death. But why would LeGore, who was so proud of his aloof mastery that he hadn't even descended to lead his own men into the Smoky River fracas, go out and personally hunt down a harmless, insignificant character like Bonnick? The only likely answer lay in LeGore's immense egoism. He had warned Bonnick not to sell out, and apparently the latent savagery of his nature had forced him to kill Bonnick as a measure of retributive revenge.

"I know the kind," mused Joe. "He's a white savage. Nothing on two legs is more dangerous. Probably he played with Bonnick before he killed the poor devil — made him sweat blood and feel the fear of death before it came. Yeah, that's what he would do."

There was a small hitch in this train of evidence. Bonnick had been shot down at some time around four o'clock. Three hours later LeGore was in Smoky River on a different horse. Where had that change been made, and for what reason? One thing sure, LeGore hadn't had time to go back to Plaza. Circumstances pointed to the renegade meeting his party somewhere along the main road and following them to Smoky River.

"He wouldn't change ponies to hide his part in the killing. He don't care who knows it as far as I can judge. Mebbe he wanted to rest the barefoot pony for a piece of work to come, like this business ahead. And what calls him over to Smoky River now?"

Much later in the night he stopped for a breathing spell and a cigarette. Then he pressed on, gradually turning southward to strike the road. Meanwhile he gave up trying to fathom LeGore's purposes. Such types were moved by primitive and contradictory passions. They did things because the ruthless push of their instincts made them. If LeGore meant to harass Smoky River again, it was because of some savage thirst that had to be slaked; he was a law unto himself.

Joe sat up and reined in to listen. Off there in the west small echoes were breaking and rolling down the land. They bore up singly and in small bursts, swelled and faded, and finally came after spaced intervals. Joe looked to the north star to verify his own location. Unless he was mistaken those shots didn't come from Smoky River but north of the town. What was north? In all the stretch of country from the canyon to the county seat he knew of but one ranch — Foshay's. The thought supplied everything else; he dropped his spurs and raced ahead.

"Ain't satisfied with killing Foshay, that black-heart! He's got to wreck all that Foshay owned. I ought to've guessed it."

A point of light, nearer than he thought the fighting to be, broke the black curtain. At first it was a thin, wavering blob of yellow, fixed to one location. But as Joe watched, he saw the light creep outward and follow several jagged routes up to the sky. So for a while it grew by moderate progression, cracking the darkness with its splaying fingers of increasing crimson; elsewhere another point of light appeared — some outhouse set to flames. The greater and lesser fires presently merged into one glow, and of a sudden the horizon was split by a raging red shield, the roar of which raced across the desert to strike the approaching Joe. It was a torch that illumined the country all around and in this angry glow Joe saw a line of riders race around from the opposite side of the fire, tarry a moment, and string out northward toward the canyon country.

Within a few minutes figures afoot crossed the light, ineffectually struggling against the blaze; Foshay's ranch hands, Joe guessed, returning, after being driven away. The heat of the fire touched his cheeks and he fell within the fringe of light, a little wary of being mistaken for some of LeGore's party. The group of ranch hands grew larger, all watching the wall of flames, and it wasn't until he had approached to within a hundred feet of them that he was discovered. Guns rose against him; he lifted one hand and closed up the interval.

He counted ten in the group. One stocky man, brick red and bearing the deep furrows of futile anger on his cheeks, came up to the pony and pulled the reins out of Joe's hand.

"Who're you?" he challenged. "What the hell you doing around here this time of night?"

"Don't get excited. Some of you boys saw me in Smoky River yesterday with my partner. LeGore took him into camp. I'm on their trail. Anybody hurt?"

Another man came forward.

"Yeah, I saw you two buzzards on the hotel porch last evening when hell busted loose. And I didn't see you getting your feet wet none. What was you so proud about? Sounds like a lousy frame-up to me. Mean to sit there and tell us you're fogging LeGore all by yourself? That's a damn lie. Nobody would do a trick so foolish."

"I'm trailing LeGore," murmured Joe, "because he's got my partner tied into double-bow knots. Anything funny about that? As for yesterday, you bet we kept out of the gunplay. So did a lot of other boys in Smoky River likewise. Why blame strangers for being peaceable when you fellows that lived here all your life knuckled down after a brace of shots and waved a yellow flag?"

"Yellow, uh?"

But Joe was not a man to back up when he got hostile; and Smoky River's easy surrender had irritated him.

"Yellow is what I said. You men were scattered all over town, you had LeGore's men badly hipped. It would've been a hard scrap and you'd of lost men in the bargain, but if you'd had any guts you would've shot that outfit off the street when they killed Foshay cold. What're you proud about, anyhow?"

"Mebbe," chimed in someone else, "you don't know the whole story, stranger."

"I know enough to keep my mouth closed," snapped Joe. "While you fellows were laying around Smoky River and wondering what to do next me and my partner broke into Plaza and had a good look. Don't try to teach your grandma how to suck eggs. And you ain't got any room to get hardboiled. So calm down. Anybody hurt here?"

They took it with poor grace, sullenly silent. But the tall man sitting above them had an air of authority and wisdom that struck home, like some schoolmaster disciplining a set of unruly youngsters. Joe Breedlove had spent too many years accumulating experience not to understand a situation such as this. "I was asking — " he began.

A puncher came racing around the snoring funnel of flame, waving his hands at the crowd. "Say, where's Miss Alice?"

The crowd started and swung to a man, someone yelled. "She run for the icehouse!"

"I know, but she ain't there now! Didn't one of you gooks ride around and haul her into the saddle? I saw somebody — !"

"Saw what? Why, jumping Jupiter — "

"Well, I'm telling you, she ain't back of the place!"

"It musta been LeGore who got around to that icehouse!"

"Who's Miss Alice?" demanded Joe.

"Foshay's girl!" yelled the puncher who still held his reins. The sweltering heat of the burning house rolled toward them and Joe's pony began backing away.

"Of all the prize halfwits," grunted Joe and jerked the reins clear of the detaining fists. "Cut out this jawing match, and start hunting! Circle around, look in the corrals and sheds. If she ain't to be found, come back here with your horses. Hurry up! Good gravy, I wouldn't hire none of you slick ears to split my kindling! Move!"

He made a wide detour of the fire to keep the horse from jumping through its skin, but he beat the Foshay punchers to the corrals by a wide margin. It was as light as full day and he saw nothing of the girl; galloping in the direction of the barn, and wondering how the incendiary torch had missed it, he passed the icehouse and its open door. There was a set of hoof tracks around it that he came near neglecting. The next instant some memory struck him between the eyes, and he whirled about and bent far down from the saddle. Bent and rose again, swinging to intercept the Foshay crew.

"LeGore's got her!" he yelled. "Those tracks by the icehouse belong to his horse — barefoot tracks. Come on!"

He swept by them and circled the desert until he intercepted the trail of the departing renegade bunch. Tracing it to the far edge of the firelight, he made a guess that the arrow-straight course leading northward indicated LeGore's intention of holing up in the canyon country. That would bring them right by the front door of the little cabin he and Indigo had bought; and a curious, unrelated thought came to him. The beans he had left simmering on the stove yesterday morning would be burnt black and totally unfit for human consumption.

"And I figured me and Indigo was settling down for a peaceful old age," he muttered. "If LeGore puts a match to that cabin on his way by, I'll just naturally cut his heart out."

Whatever the defects of the Foshay crew, he could find no fault in the manner they flung themselves along the trail and overtook him. He had to check them from going by.

"One of you boys will have to stick behind and wait for the Smoky River crowd to come up. These tracks aim for the canyon. LeGore's probably going to make a camp in the hills. The town boys have got to know we're ahead so's they won't bust into us with a mess of lead. Who stays?"

There was no volunteer. Joe grunted impatiently and singled out the most youthful face in the party. "You stay. When they come, tell 'em we're ahead and waiting. If we have to leave the canyon, I'll leave a man behind to show 'em the way."

"How do you know anybody's coming from Smoky River?" countered the lad. "They dunno what's taking place here."

"They'll see fire in the sky, and if that don't bring every man-jack on the run, then Smoky River is dead enough to make a buzzard hurry by. You drop back, son. And while you're waiting, put them two led horses I left behind in the barn. Water 'em and fork down some hay. Come on, gents!"

They raced on, hearing the sudden crash of the ranchhouse roof falling in. The fire burned more fiercely and the glow rose higher to the heavens. The Foshay bunch, stung by the disaster to their outfit, kept looking back to that torch of wrath, muttering sullen threats of vengeance. Joe nodded to himself in the darkness; they were whipping themselves to a fighting pitch, they were forgetting for the moment the specter of LeGore's name, a name that had the power of going on ahead of the outlaw and cowing people by its intangible threat. Smoky River had long been undermined by it, the town's courage had been sapped from day to day until it had crumbled and surrendered after half a dozen shots and the sight of LeGore sitting aloof above the powder smoke. These boys riding with Joe suffered from the same handicap; LeGore had them spooked, which was not to be wondered at, for Joe had felt a little spooky himself when he first saw the stiff, gray figure of the man.

Yet he knew how this vicious machine had been built up and he knew how it could be destroyed. Along the back trail of his life, Joe Breedlove had seen the same thing. First it was the story of a man stepping beyond the bounds of law, establishing the fact of his own hard character. Most of the men belonging to this type were soon cut down by a retributive bullet, but those who escaped it soon acquired a legend of power beyond their worth, a legend that peaceful citizens helped to strengthen and glorify by oft-repeated tales.

Folks like to put a glamour around the outlaw, as they had done since the days of Robin Hood and before. A toleration was established and under this kind of protection the renegade flourished and grew more destructive until toleration passed into fear and men avoided coming into collision with him. Other renegades banded in with him, and presently there was a force in the country stronger than the established law of the community. This was the history of Slash LeGore.

But there was no outlaw as ferocious and impregnable as the legend surrounding him; and there was no community that could not, by mass action, kill off what they had helped to create through their own neglect. He who lived by the sword died by the sword. Joe knew that if he could rouse the men of Smoky River and the country around he could break up LeGore's band and bring the gray, impassive figure to bay. Then he would match guns with the man. He wasn't sure of the result but he knew that meeting was as certain as the fixed stars in the sky.

Thinking thus, Joe led the small party onward across the desert. The glare of the burning ranch subsided, the yellow outline grew smaller; and at last he saw ahead the mouth of the canyon yawning dimly through the midnight pall. The river swung out of the fissure, murmuring against the stones and a slow breeze sighed between the straggling pines. Behind them lay the open desert; before them was the hint of mystery, the promise of trouble. Joe sensed the slackening of spirit amongst the men and he stopped; if ever he was to beat LeGore and smash the evil ring around the renegade, he had to establish for once and all his own supremacy.

"You lads don't seem to be so chipper. An hour ago you seemed willing to spit in a cougar's face. LeGore got the Indian sign on this outfit? If you're afraid, turn around and go home. I started out alone and I reckon I can finish alone."

"You a-trying to put the hooks in us?" grunted one of the party. "I have took about all the dirty slams off you which I'm gonna. Who told you Smoky River didn't have no guts? When this brawl is over, brother, I'm sure going to climb your frame and see what grows on top. You go to hell!"

Joe grinned to himself. "Well, that's what I wanted to find out. I ain't aiming to bust into something and find myself all alone. Somewhere up this canyon LeGore's camping. We're pushing right on till we find sign. This is ticklish business and we've got to move light. No unnecessary sound. Our business is to surround the camp and wait for the rest of the bunch to come ahead. It'll be daylight by then. Meanwhile, no shooting. And I want it understood right here that this is my Christmas party. What I say goes. Does that sink in?"

"Cover a lot of territory, don't you?"

"Some plenty," was Joe's laconic answer. "And I've had lots of years to cover it in, too. Stick by me tonight, and I'll show you a few things they forgot to put in the books."

"Yeah? What's this — a Fourth of July speech? Go ahead and we'll show you how to fight."

Joe was not normally given to talking about himself, nor would he have done it with these boys had he not wanted to rouse them to a proper state of hostility. So he pushed his barbs a little deeper.

"If any of you dudes have got cold feet, better drop out now. Just remember, there ain't any outlaw born that can't be knocked out of the saddle with one good bullet. None of 'em wear iron shirts. From here on we ride two and two. Keep away from the gravel. When I push the man nearest me once, that means stop. If I nudge him twice, that means come ahead. When we stop, don't try to start until you hear from me, no matter how long I'm gone. Now let's proceed and see how good you are at something besides mouth fighting."

"You'll sure eat that!" snapped somebody.

"You better grow up first," advised Joe. "Come on."

They strung along behind him. The canyon walls swept down on either side and the shadows crowded more thickly around. Necessarily they made some amount of noise, but the swash and ripple of the river absorbed these marks of advance, and Joe pressed on at a brisk walk until he had gone about a half mile. There was a little butte crowding out toward the river at one spot and, as he remembered from the previous trip out, it stood about three hundred yards from the Bonnick cabin. Rounding this, he brought the group to a halt and started to the front. No light broke through the shadows.

It was possible, of course, that LeGore had avoided the canyon and taken to the high ground. Even possible the outlaw had curved away short of the hill country and struck back for Plaza San Felipe. But Joe was working on a strong hunch. LeGore was packing Indigo around, he believed, for the sole purpose of towing himself into a trap. That being so, it didn't sound reasonable to Joe that LeGore would double back to Plaza. And after burning the Foshay ranch and abducting the girl, the gray renegade, it seemed to him, would streak directly for strong shelter. Such was this hill country; and the most convenient entrance to it ran along the river.

"No use trying to reason out that man's way of doing business," he said to himself. "He's apt to do anything. If I got a hunch, I'd better play it. Something tells me I'd better have a little look at that cabin."

He relayed this idea sibilantly back, chose the nearest man, and with him crawled onward afoot. "May be some sort of a trap yonder," he whispered to his side. "Good place for one. Stay right by me."

A hundred yards farther they got down on their stomachs. Five minutes of this labor brought them within sighting distance of the cabin. The peaked outline of it was hardly more than discernible and they could make out nothing but the yard or barn behind. Progressing at a slower and more careful gait, they finally rested within stone's throw of the cabin door. When the partners had left it the morning before, it had been open; at present it was closed.

Joe pressed his companion's head flat to the sandy soil. Something moved out there in the yard, moved slowly. A minute sound rose above the river's rippling, a faint bulk broke away from the cabin's outline and stepped to the water's edge, falling prone. LeGore's picket taking a drink. Was this fellow alone here? And where was LeGore camping? The aide moved nervously. Joe stopped that with a poke of his elbow and relapsed to his immense, Indianlike patience.

Presently the picket had enough of water, rose and walked to the cabin. For a moment he seemed to be exploring the night, testing out his senses, keening the air for trouble. Then he passed inside the cabin; a match glow made a dim, fragmentary struggle against the darkness and went out. Within that space of time Joe had risen and crossed the interval, standing with his back to the cabin wall and the muzzle of his gun lifted high. The picket sighed and swore; a pan jangled against the floor. This seemed to disturb the picket, for he came quickly out the door. Joe's gun barrel felled him senseless to the ground.

The Foshay puncher sprang forward, muttering, "Bashed him! I heard that smack!"

"Shut up!" grunted Joe. "Ain't you got the brains God give you! Shut up and stay where I put you. Woods may be full of these gents."

He slid away from the cabin. Up against the corral he found a single horse tethered. With that reassurance he went back. "You hit for the bunch. Tell 'em to come along on foot. Leave one man with the horses. Tell him to pull the brutes inside of that little point so's he won't be blocking the trail. He's to watch for the Smoky River gang also."

The puncher retreated. Joe returned to the outlaw's horse and took the reata. With that he bound the prone and unconscious figure, stripped him of his gunbelt and lugged him to the corral where he ran a few extra loops around the bottom bar. His searching fist found a rock slightly less than egg-size; he jammed it in the outlaw's mouth and finished the homely gag with the outlaw's own neckpiece. Then he led the horse into the barn and tied it. Going back to the cabin, he found the Foshay crew waiting in complete silence.

"Slipped up on me, uh?" he mused. "Well, you're getting some better. Now if you'll just practice keeping your traps closed, we may do something yet. Come ahead. We're beginning to smell fresh tracks."

A few yards beyond the cabin was the ford. He stopped again and knelt in the sand, brushing it with his palm. There were indentations here, whether recent or old he had no means of judging. Yet slightly to one side his fingers touched a damp track and from this he gathered at least one of LeGore's party had crossed the river and later recrossed it. The main bunch hadn't traveled that way. That left two trails open: over the ridge behind the cabin or straight up the canyon. Still swayed by his hunch, Joe chose the canyon.

During the week he and Indigo had lived in the canyon they had explored the country with a casual interest and Joe knew that directly ahead the river began to buckle up and twist like an angry snake while the paralleling ridges climbed toward the sky with very little slope. The farther he walked the greater was the reverberation of the not far distant rapids; the miniature strip of bottom land petered out and they curled single file around a yard-wide shelving. The river turned abruptly from north to east and after a few hundred feet struck another right angle projection of the canyon wall that deflected it again.

Ahead, on the opposite side of the water a faint blood glow flickered against the face of a spray-damp cliff. Joe punched the man behind him as a signal to halt and went on alone. Presently, belly-flat on the damp rock, he peered around another jutting elbow. But this stretch was pitch black; that reflected camp fire was around still another bend. Quietly he retreated and drew the punchers into a compact little group.

"Anybody know this canyon? What's it lead into? Any way out from above? This ain't the only way of coming or going, is it?"

There was a long, reflective silence. Someone finally supplied a dubious answer.

" 'Taint country we boys explore much. Far's I know it just keeps getting narrower and narrower. Goes plumb into the bowels of the earth, I reckon. Cliff sides is a hundred feet high from here on, but there's a place where you might spit across the drink. Dunno's there's any other way of getting out."

"That don't make sense," grunted Joe. "LeGore wouldn't put himself into a trap. Must be a way out from the other end, or up the sides."

"LeGore's a crazy man."

"Yeah? Well, son, when you're as crazy as LeGore you won't be working for forty and found. One thing is mighty certain, if there is any trail from either side or the other end, he's got it guarded. Must have guards along the rims, too. He wouldn't let himself be shot out from above."

"Ain't hardly no way of getting onto the rims from the hill sides. Plenty tough, far's

I can remember. Folks don't ram around this country unless they got trouble. Me, I never had that kind of trouble."

"Well," decided Joe. "I'm going to wiggle ahead and see what I can. You boys sit tight. Better drop one man back some to pick up the Smoky River fellows. If any of them know a way of getting onto the rims, they'd better start before it gets any later. But don't start any rumpus until I get back. They've got a girl and they've got my partner. We can't sling lead into 'em. Which I guess LeGore knows pretty well and is using it for a hole card. Sit tight."

He retraced his way to the first shelving and after a long wait in the almost opaque blackness, pushed himself on, gained what seemed like a little indentation in the cliff side and rose away from the river's edge. By every known rule LeGore ought to have a sentry stationed here, yet the passing moments revealed nothing to him; if there was any sound of such a sentry's moving about, it was entirely lost in the rush of water piling against the boulder-strewn channel.

By indefinite degrees he groped along the clammy face of the cliff as it drew him in a semicircle, first farther from the water and then back to it again. Another narrow ledge lay in front of him. Considering his chances carefully, he at last stepped onto the ledge, fully expecting to see the campfire bursting through the black from the next indentation in the canyon wall. But he saw no such fire. Instead there appeared to be a long and tortuous trail around a considerable bend; and from the stronger glow on the opposite wall — a glow that never penetrated the depths of the canyon — he guessed there must be some rather wide beach deeply inset in the rocks at the end of the bend.

The canyon had so far promised everything and revealed nothing. Yet having reached this parlous situation he was in no humor to turn back. If there was a trail up the canyon wall, he believed the outlaw campfire might show it; and from that he might get some idea of flanking LeGore. Therefore, he pressed on, wanting to hurry but held back by the uncertainty of what lay to the front. The ledge was an endless succession of jagged turns; once he struck his head sharply against an overhanging rock and fell to his knees on the damp trail. A stringer of spray shot up to his face. Rising, he touched his gun butt and crowded nearer the wall; and at that moment he heard a man's prolonged, full-throated challenge bear up over the boom and slash off the rapids. One of the renegades was coming back from the camp ahead.

"Dan — hey, Dan!"

Joe stopped dead and flung himself about. His mind raced ahead to the stark possibilities left him — to retreat, the river, or the cliff. Even the retreat was impossible, for there was an answering hail from the opposite direction, near enough to tell Joe he was trapped on the tortuous ledge. For a moment he debated sliding into the water and hanging by his fingers. That alternative he rejected; the tempestuous current would haul him instantly away, and he doubted if life would last the length of that smashing strip of river. As for attempting to close in on either of the advancing renegades and catching him off guard — that too he threw out as the grim and ultimate resort of necessity. Like most plainsmen, Joe feared the water and he could not quite meet the idea of deliberately pushing another into a strangling death.

"Dan, you comin'?"

"Hi!"

They were but a few yards to either side of him. Joe's long arms reached up against the rock face and brushed the promise of a fissure just beyond reach. He bent at the knees and threw his whole body into the succeeding jump; his fingers slid along a jagged indentation and, every muscle snapping to an immense pressure, he hauled himself head-high with this break in the rock, let go with one arm and reached again. The fissure took a slanting course upward, met another that angled like a staircase and fell into a slight pocket. Six feet above the ledge, Joe braced himself, with one foot jammed here and an arm clutching there, all spread out like a crab while the river seemed to send up its reverberations to break him loose. The renegades had joined directly below him and were talking. So he hung, feeling the fingers of his left hand aching from the strain of too insecure a grip.

Chapter 6

The meeting of the pair was brief and laconic.

"Chief says for me to take your place, Dan. You go back to the fire."

"What's up?"

"Nothing, as far as I know. Heard anything of the little man's pardner? Chief figures he'll be snooping around."

"Nope. He ain't fool enough to stick his nose into this layout."

"Chief figures he's pretty hard. Seems to want him some bad. Well, go get your coffee. Dam' wet place to hang around. Think I'll walk back a piece towards the cabin."

They passed each other and retreated along the ledge. Joe's left hand had gone numb and, shifting to relieve it of pressure, he sought around for a better grip. The rock face seemed to slant inward and there were several fissures breaking across it. Rising higher from the ledge he secured an easier position and stopped to consider the situation. If that new sentry went back toward the cabin, he would pass the punchers waiting a few feet off the trail. He wondered if they would have sense enough to keep still or if they would challenge, thinking it to be himself returning.

"Maybe they got brains enough to figure that if the dude doesn't sound off, it can't be me. Then they'll clamp him down and I sure hope they don't let him get started on any gunplay."

It was in the lap of the gods. Meanwhile he had another idea. The rock face seemed to offer passable ascent. Once he got high enough, he could command a good view of LeGore's camp, and it was even possible that he might arrive at the rim and find some trail going down from above the camp which would later permit the Smoky River bunch to lay a ring around LeGore. The more he thought about it, the surer Joe was that the renegade chief would never allow himself to be boxed in a blind canyon. There must be some other way of entrance and departure. Thinking this, he started up.

The farther he climbed the greater was the incline of the cliff and the easier his labor. At a distance he judged to be fifty feet he crawled to a rounding summit and found himself looking directly into the indented beach below. A great fire blazed there, throwing its full crimson glow against the sullen backdrop of the rocks and out into the charging strip of water. He counted about thirty of LeGore's party in the light; the other ten apparently were out on guard. LeGore himself was not visible; neither was Indigo, though Joe swept the beach with careful eye. But the girl sat on a saddle by the fire, looking into it with a fixity apparent even from the distance.

The sight of her in such somber surroundings, caught helplessly up in LeGore's mesh and guarded by the dregs of the country, roused Joe's full wrath. He had seen many evil, barbaric things in his varied life and he knew how deep was man's inhumanity to man, yet he never ceased to be shocked and outraged when women suffered from the raw cruelties of Western life. His humorously gentle and pessimistic philosophy made allowances for almost every human error, but there was in him no sympathy for such a thing as this. LeGore had passed beyond the bounds of Joe's code; LeGore deserved nothing better than the death of a wild animal.

For another minute or two he swept the outer fringes of light. It appeared there were small galleries worn into the side of the cliff from the ancient friction of the river, and he guessed LeGore had bundled Indigo into one of them. Turning, he crawled along the surface of the promontory and saw the mouth of a yard-wide alley leading up through the cliff. Logs and boulders choked it. Tediously he crept over all this, making as little noise as he could; then he was climbing again and at last arrived at the canyon's east rim. Pines stood along the rim. Exploring through them, he came to a barren area and out of past experience he crept around the edge of the area to find the trail that usually fell into such open spaces — trails made by the forest creatures going down to drink and later usurped by man.

He found such a trail and turned northward on it, traveling two or three hundred feet, guiding himself by the fire glow that appeared now and then through the brush. When the pathway began to dip and circle back to the river, he abated his speed and swung into the trees. This entrance to the canyon bottom was too broad and plain to be left unguarded.

But though he waited until his patience ran out, nothing moved along the trail. The posse from Smoky River would have reached the scene by now and daylight was not far away. He could not afford too much caution; possibly the guard was posted farther down the hills where the trail began. So he took the winding course before him and crawled another hundred yards along a rather stiff grade. Presently he stood by the river, looking at LeGore's campfire from the opposite direction.

Knowing this, it was time to go back and locate his posse. Proximity to LeGore, however, stirred his curiosity. He wanted to find out just where Indigo lay; and there was in his mind another idea. As long as Indigo and the girl were captives, it would not be possible to blast LeGore out of his position. The renegade, even if surrounded, held the whip. But if Indigo were far enough away from the light, and further, if the girl might leave the fire, then — But, being a practical man, he dismissed this hope of perfect fortune; however, being also a gambler at heart and realizing that the breaks of luck came most often to the man who waited for them, he pressed his body against the cliff and stepped nearer the camp.

The irregular outline of the cliff shielded him. He was still in dense shadows, yet he could see, whenever he sidled away from the cliff, the men of the outfit moving idly around the fire. He likewise began to make out an occasional figure wrapped in blankets beneath the overhang; and while he surveyed the scene, LeGore came forward to the fire and bent over the girl. The rush and boom of the river drowned out whatever he said. Alice Foshay shook her head without looking up. LeGore spread his arms wide apart, he pointed to the cliff. The girl rose and moved around the fire, chin rising defiantly. At that, LeGore shrugged his shoulders and started away.

Joe closed in beside the rocks again and moved in. He thought he heard a sound foreign to the river, but he had been misled several times by the sheeting of spray against the rocks and he disregarded this faint echo. It nearly led him into fatal error. Not until his own sure inner sense warned him did he throw himself flat to the hard ground; a horse and rider galloped by from the trail behind, close enough to fling gravel in his face, and up to the fire. The man dropped off, confronting LeGore. He pointed to the rim above and then along the trail leading down the canyon. LeGore's arm rose, and all at once the camp was up and stirring restlessly. A dozen men drew apart and moved toward the narrow ledge along the down trail. A twist of LeGore's wrist sent as many back toward Joe.

The girl's white face flashed in the light and she circled the fire, putting herself nearer the cliff. Then a flat report smashed through the river's roar, followed by a steady volley of shot that checked the renegade party which had drawn into the down-trail ledge. The compact group faltered, split apart; three of the men fell and the rest came racing back. LeGore's tall frame shifted away from the light and the fire was kicked apart, trampled down. The glow died from the cliff walls, but in the last dull shower of sparks Joe saw the girl racing toward him. The firing became general. Joe left his covert and jumped forward to intercept Foshay's daughter before the canyon's pall had swallowed her.

As it was, he nearly missed her. She knew that she would be followed and when the last of the light had gone she twisted from side to side. Only the fact that the beach narrowed considerably brought the two shoulder to shoulder. Joe's outstretched fingers brushed her dress. He turned and caught her, taking a severe beating across the face before he could make himself understood.

"Hold on — wait a minute! I'm the partner of that little fellow LeGore's got roped up. I — "

"Let me go! I'll kill you!"

"All right, all right. Just calm down a little, ma'am. We'll get clear. But I want to know where they got my partner. We'll get out of this. Just trust me some. Come over here against the cliff. Flat against it. That's right. Where've they got my partner? I ain't been able to see him."

"What's your name?"

"Joe Breedlove."

She ceased struggling, the breath choked in her throat and she fell to coughing. Apparently the Smoky River contingent had arrived, for the firing from that direction took on the tone of a general engagement. So far LeGore's outfit hadn't drawn a gun.

"I — I heard them talk about you!" she whispered. "The little man is tied to a loose saddle and he's sitting in the hollow of the cliff, almost directly opposite the fire! How can I get out of here?"

"They ain't going to light that fire again," muttered Joe. "I think I'll just amble in among 'em and look for Indigo."

A stray bullet chipped the rock near by; another sang into the water's edge. Joe put himself in front of the girl and pushed her back toward the trail. LeGore had something up his sleeve; it was too quiet there on the beach. Joe groped around until he found the mouth of the trail leading up the cliff; for a moment he paused to listen, then guided her into it.

"Now we've got to run up this at a dead gallop. Should a pony come down, we'll get knocked galley west and barn high."

The injunction was unnecessary. Foshay's daughter ran away from him. Sliding across the loose rubble, he lost sound of her and wondered if she was going to plunge aimlessly into the brush and lose herself. After the last forty-eight hours of tragedy he wouldn't have blamed her any. Yet when he got to the top of the rim, wet with sudden sweat and badly winded, a soft hand touched him and drew him aside from the trail. Ten years younger and Joe would have felt his pride somewhat lacerated. As it was he absorbed the crisp air and felt thankful she was out of LeGore's claws.

"No busted down fellow like me ought to take to nighthawking. I ain't as good a man as I wish I was. You're safe right here, ma'am. Just stay in the brush till I come back. I've got to go and see what I can do about Indigo — "

She caught at his coat. "No — you never will make it! It isn't that I'm afraid, but LeGore will kill you if he ever catches you down there! He told your friend and myself during the ride tonight that you'd follow and that he'd put a bullet through your heart. He hates you, Mr. Breedlove. He believes you are pulling the country together against him."

"Which is a plumb nice compliment, ain't it?" drawled Joe. "But Indigo's in trouble — "

"He won't hurt your partner. It is only men who set themselves against him that he hates. He's a cruel, heartless savage!"

"Yeah? Well, he don't know much about Indigo if he thinks that little hunk of dynamite can't pull the pillars over his head when the chance comes. Well, I got my wind back and it ain't so blamed far from daylight. I'll tackle it. In case I don't show up — "

Riders drummed up the trail and turned the curve of the rim, smashing the overhanging brush in their passage. Joe pushed the girl farther back and listened to the beat of hoofs going by. A shrill yell sailed like a javelin through the night and broke off at the climax of its high pitch; then the last rider was by and the forest dust rolled out. Joe never swore in front of a woman, but he did so now in full, overflowing measure. "That's Indigo's yell. And they belted it out of him! I'll bust that bunch to hell and gone before I'm finished!"

"I'm sorry," murmured the girl.

"Well, they've skinned out, the whole pack.

Let's hunt a way through this jungle."

Eastward in the sky was the promise of first dawn. They took the trail and followed it, crossing open stretches and turning down from slope to slope. The river's roar fell behind, the dust of the renegade band's passage still clung to the air. A quarter hour later they were at the bottom of a fairly open draw. Joe stopped to orient himself.

"Left goes north, right goes south. What's out yonder I dunno. I'm all mixed up. New country to me. But we'll tackle the right trail and see what's what. No wonder LeGore felt safe. But what he ever come into that canyon for in the first place is beyond me."

"To draw you on," said the girl. "He told me that."

"Oh, shucks," protested Joe, "he wouldn't fog clear over the country just for that."

But Foshay's daughter had good cause to know the renegade's mind. "He will do anything if it fits in with his purpose."

"Then what was his purpose in taking you?" demanded Joe.

"Not to hurt me," said the girl. "Oh, I don't know what was in the back of his cruel brain. Perhaps to hurt me because I was the daughter of a man he hated and killed. But more to terrorize the country, to show folks his power."

Joe considered that over a long stretch of trail while a dim mist of light cracked the horizon. "When a man gets to living up to the stories about himself he's gone loco. Which is LeGore. He overreached himself in laying hands on you. There ain't any country, no matter how scared it might be of an outlaw, which'd stand for a play like that. Smoky River come on the run. And we'd of bagged the gent, too, if somebody hadn't got too previous about shooting."

"We will never forget it," murmured the girl. "He'll make us suffer for it." The high tide of her courage had gone out, leaving her discouraged and trembling.

Joe put one hand under her arm and pointed to a bald slope dawning through the pale shadows. "Don't figure that, ma'am. Showdown is sure coming. Let's tackle that hill. Has a sort of familiar look to me."

When they reached the top they saw Bonnick's cabin sitting peacefully by the river's edge. Horses moved in the corrals and there was a lantern bobbing across the yard. Joe studied it a moment and led the girl down the slope. They hadn't quite reached the cabin when a long file of riders came out from the upper reaches of the canyon. Smoky River men dropped to the ground. A redheaded chap flung himself toward Alice Foshay with a strange cry in his throat. Joe turned abruptly and sought out a familiar face — that of a Foshay puncher he had earlier led into trouble.

"What was the idea of slinging lead so damn early?" he demanded.

"Good grief, friend! We figured you was a gone goose!"

"How'd you manage to get Miss Alice?"

"Suffering catfish, where you been? We throwed lead because there didn't seem nothing else to do. No, that ain't exactly right. We was all together and waiting for you when we bumped into some galoot from LeGore's bunch. He rode right into the back of us. That primed off the fireworks."

"Well, we give LeGore a scare, didn't we? He's flew the coop. How'd he get out?"

Joe rolled a cigarette while all this aimless conversation went on, hearing a letdown of tension in their voices. "Out the back door," he grunted. "Same way I went out. You don't suppose he was fool enough to walk into a blind alley, do you?"

"Well, we made him jar loose of Miss Alice. He ain't so doggone powerful."

"He's got my partner," observed Joe. "Let's hit for town."

"All over but the shouting," said somebody.

Joe's temper flared. "Like hell! You birds ain't done nothing yet. You're going to bust that outfit before we're finished. Don't get no callouses from patting your own backs."

A middle-aged fellow drew up. "Your name's Breedlove, ain't it? Yeah, well I found this note hangin' to a pole stuck in the ground by their campfire. Looks like LeGore's whistling up your alley."

Joe took the note and read it:

> Breedlove: If you want your pardner alive, come to Plaza and get him.
>
> Slash LeGore

Another Smoky Hill man was reading the note over Joe's shoulder. He drew back, sighing. "I grew up with Slash, Breedlove. I know him like a brother. He means that."

Joe said nothing but in the violet light of morning his lean and tired face was drawn to savage furrows. The gentle, happy partner had turned to a side of his nature he had spent his life in suppressing. When he stepped up to the saddle and rode ahead of the party toward Smoky River, he was a blood killer.

Chapter 7

It was Joe Breedlove's sincere belief that he was by nature a spectator of life and that he was happiest when observing human nature from the sidelines. But like many another man his theories varied a great deal from actual practice. No matter how often he repeated that peace was his motto, or that he wished to be a leader in no cause, the turning wheel of events continually threw him up above the crowd. There was something about the calm, tall figure that inspired confidence at first glance. In his casual drawl was the melody of leadership; upon his shrewd face was the stamp of mellow experience. No matter how humbly he trailed along with men, his very nature sooner or later put him at the head of the party. He couldn't help it. Every mile and year of his life was marked with hard and fast friends who, coming into contact with him, swore allegiance.

So it was now. A leaderless Smoky River felt his slow and rugged character and turned to him. It was not by accident that when the posse rode into town during the forenoon, he was at the front of it; nor was it accident that those who had been through the night's turbulent affair closed around him and waited for what he had to say. He had much to say but, studying them carefully, he saw this was no time to say it. He knew men too well to press beyond a certain limit. They were weary and hungry. The fighting spirit was gone out of them. Some, he understood, were afraid of the night's work and Slash LeGore's retributive wrath; some were satisfied with having defied the outlaw and wrested the girl from his control. The still-captive Indigo meant nothing to them. Therefore, Joe shrewdly kept away from his subject.

"We all need sleep and we all need grub. Meanwhile, you boys stick close to town. We're not finished yet."

The red-headed youth had taken Alice Foshay into the hotel and he caught only the last sentence. "You bet we ain't," he muttered. "There's a long row of potatoes to hoe."

Joe marked the redhead for his lieutenant at that moment. Turning, he stabled his horses, having picked up the two left at Foshay's ranch, and went to get his first solid meal in a day and a half. After that he walked wearily into a hotel room and slept.

When he woke it was dark and there came from the street the sound of freighters moving out of town. A fresh breeze scoured through the room from window to an open door; and the young redheaded puncher sat in a chair, smoking a cigarette. Joe let his muscles idle a moment, wondering if he were growing old. Five years earlier and no man would have gotten into his room without rousing him. Each year brought its stealthy handicap to the body, took the sharp edge from the senses, spoiled the fine adjustment of nerve and eye. The angry fighting flame would be the same when he met LeGore face to face, the same destructive impulse would drive his arm toward the gun. His mind would race ahead as usual and nothing would melt the cold sheathing around his resolution to kill. But as fast as he was, he knew he could never match the speed of his younger years. And, almost critically aloof, he wondered about LeGore.

"Well, boy?"

The redhead started and swore. "Judas, you gave me a scare! Lying so still I didn't know you had woke. I was waiting."

"Anything worrying you?"

"I wanted to thank you," was the redhead's gruff statement. "For getting Alice out of that jam. Me, I was three parts crazy last night. I'd of walked into that camp if the boys hadn't cussed me back to some sense. Just you remember this — Alice and me is under debt to you. It ain't never going to be paid off. Can't be. Too big a debt. But, hell, you know what I mean. Day or night, from now on, you got a call on me."

Joe sat up and pulled on his boots. Rolling a cigarette he struck a match, his eyes a profound, shimmering blue. "Thanks, son. Guess you'll be marrying that little lady, won't you?"

"Yeah."

"Stick fast to her, boy. There ain't — " The words dwindled out through the smoke. The tall partner sighed, thinking back through the years to that time when he cherished something more than memories. "There ain't much place in the scheme of things for a single man. He's a lonely brute. He's incomplete. The Lord never meant folks to live alone."

"We ain't getting married," interposed the redhead, "until LeGore is taken care of. No peace for me as long as he's around. I closeherded 'em this afternoon to keep strays from loping away. You got an idea?"

"Yeah," murmured Joe.

"Then, for God's sake, spring it before Smoky River starts jumping at its shadow again! Me, I don't rate big enough around this place to organize any party. Foshay could've done it. You can do it. Nobody else. They'll listen to you. They know what you went and done single-handed. There's fifty men here able to knock hell out of LeGore's bunch if they only took a notion."

"All of 'em to be trusted?" was Joe's mild query.

"I wasn't counting the gents I don't trust."

Joe got up and, followed by the redhead, went down to the street. "I'm going for a bite to eat," said Joe. "You collect all the boys in the hotel lobby. I want to talk to them. And if there's anybody in the crowd you don't trust, just sift over and stand next to that party so I can see who it is. I've got an idea that'll work, but we can't take along any dead weight."

"You bet," grunted the redhead, and pivoted away. Joe strolled on to the restaurant.

He dallied over his meal, which was a strange perversion of a lifelong habit to eat and be off; he savored his food as if he found in it unexpected pleasures, while his mind revolved around other thoughts, some reminiscent of youth, some recalling the great duels along his tempestuous career. And always these thoughts led him back with a gripping directness to the stiff, gray figure of LeGore. He would be facing LeGore before this night had run out the dark hours, that he felt as certain of as the fact of his own existence; he had known it since the very first moment of meeting. There were fixed laws of life and one of them had never failed to shape the course of his fortune: LeGore's kind and his kind were forever doomed to cross and clash. Nothing that he or the outlaw chief might do could ever change immutable destiny.

He felt no fear, his pulse ran cool and even; but he was visualizing LeGore's dead face, the iron sweep of shoulder and arm, the enormous stretch of fingers. He was even hearing LeGore's flat, restless monotone. The man embodied every element of destructive force — physical power, an egoism that rode over all weakness, a litheness of tendon and joint, and a cold nervelessness that was akin to the reptile world. He did not fear LeGore, yet he wondered as he lifted his eyes to the light, eyes which were ink blue from the pressure of his thoughts, which one of them would see morning flame over the eastern sky. He drank the last of his coffee and rose to pay the bill.

"That steak," he told the restaurant man, "will stick in my mind as the best I ever ate, brother."

"Got plenty more like it," said the other, thawing under the compliment. "You come here in the morning and I'll turn one out better yet. A man's got to eat meat. I'll hold the best in the ice box for you."

But Joe smiled, a little wistful and a little sad as he left the place. "It ain't the quality of the meat, old-timer, nor the ketchup on it. Appetite runs with time and tide. Tonight I ate a meal such as I never expect to relish again."

With that he walked along the street and into the hotel lobby to find half a hundred men waiting for him. He shouldered through and stood on the stairway above them. As he swept their faces his lean body straightened and the subdued mastery of self and circumstance came to his fine, square countenance. There was nothing hidden in Joe Breedlove. All that he was lay open. When he started to speak it was dead silent.

"As long as LeGore is alive you will never have a day of peace, you will never know what a sound sleep is. As long as he is alive you will bend to his word. What he has done is not a fraction of what he will do. He killed Foshay, wrecked this town, laid his dirty paws on a woman, and burnt a ranch. He holds my partner under the threat of blood. He believes he's got you all in mortal terror of his name. And if you think you are done with him and willing to let him alone, you are committing suicide. He has sent me a personal challenge that I am going to meet. Tonight I ride for Plaza. I want forty horses behind me to help wipe out that spawning ground of the devil."

He had never lifted his voice above a single steady beat and at the end the silence was as complete as when he began. But he knew, from the change of their eyes and the pinching-in of lip and nostril, that he had won them. He started down the steps, but stopped when he saw the redhead move through the close crowd and stand casually behind Cash Cairns. The sorrel-complexioned deputy had returned, secure in the belief that Plaza held his secret. Joe spoke again.

"I want men to follow me who've got no doubts in their minds as to what side they belong to. When we ride there won't be time for trickery and if anybody makes that mistake, he will never live to repent. It is a sorry country that has to scrap its law and go to vigilante rule, but tonight we have got to do a dirty chore and there won't be any lawyers riding with us. That is a plain warning to the wavering and the gents here who would rather fight for Plaza. I am saddling up. Those that aim to go with me, do likewise."

The redhead threw him a significant glance, and he nodded slowly as he passed through to the street. The men of Smoky River tramped solidly behind him, and when he had saddled his own pony again and rode to the street they, too, were waiting to ride. A cigarette glowed here and there along the line and an occasional sibilant phrase broke sharply through the night. Otherwise they were silent and self-contained, seeming to catch from Joe Breedlove the hint of the bitter business ahead of them. Leading them out of town, he was conscious of the fact that he had never ridden with a more seriously grim set of men.

Just beyond town he stopped. "For your information, boys, we're going to circle around Plaza and hit from yonder side. They will be waiting. They'll have guards out, but they'll be strongest at this end, thinking we'll prob'ly hit thataway. That's all I have got to say until we're ready to pour down on 'em. Now we stretch out."

They struck a steady pace eastward along

the main trail between towns, the beat of their many hoofs rising up to the dim stars, and the creak and jingle of gear making a soothing rhythm in the night. The last light of Smoky River died out, the desert took them within the cloak of its mystery. Mile after mile fell to the rear; up and down the swell of the land they galloped, close-ranked, drumming through the ruts and along the powdered dust. Presently they beat over an open bridge traversing a dry arroyo. Joe swung, the road dropped behind and they were cutting a wide circle to the north. The redhead forged abreast of Joe, kept the pace for a quarter hour and then gently pulled away and slackened speed. Presently he was abreast again, muttering a soft warning at the tall partner.

"Cairns was with us when we started, but I think he's pulled up. He heard what you said about hitting Plaza from behind. We better stop to make sure if he's gone."

"In a little while," said Joe.

"Yeah, but if he gets ahead of us and warns 'em, he can do a lot of damage."

"More good than damage," murmured Joe.

"I don't trust the man. I think he's hooked up with LeGore."

"I know he is, son. I saw him in Plaza last night talking to LeGore."

"Well, then, we had better look — "

"In a little while."

That little while stretched out to hours. A windmill's gaunt outline broke through the curtain and Joe, who had observed it the previous day, drew around to it and stopped. Beneath the solitary tower was a shallow tank of water for stock and into this the hard breathing ponies dropped their nuzzles. "Now," drawled Joe, "let's see if Cairns is among those present. Cairns!"

There was a shifting and self-inspection among the riders. "Ain't here."

"He started with us."

"Yellow dog got cold and quit."

"Quit, hell! He's fogging towards Plaza to tell LeGore!"

"Well, we're sunk, then."

"We're sunk in a hog's eye. We'll bust that joint in a thousand pieces!"

"Plaza's a big joint to knock over when it's on the watch."

"How about that, Breedlove? We got to tackle it another way, ain't we?"

"We don't ride in until about three o'clock," drawled Joe. "By that time all the folks that ain't aiming to fight against us will be in bed or up at the mines, or out of town. Which leaves LeGore's party on the street. We're about a match for his number and we won't be worrying about shooting down some harmless bystander."

"Yeah, but he's all primed to meet us at the back side."

"I never intended to go in the back side," said Joe, words floating through the still crisp air. "I wanted Cairns to hear me say that. And I wanted him to break away and tell LeGore what he heard. We go in the front way."

"Which likewise will be cluttered with LeGore's gimlet-brained assassins."

"They'll never see us till we're clean inside," countered Joe. "Leave that to me."

"Time to be going?"

"Not yet."

The party rested while the hours went along, dragging interminably for the more restless members. Midnight came and one o'clock. Joe struck a match to his watch and when the hour hand verged around toward two he swung up and led them away. This time the direction changed from north to southeast, back to the main highway. Another hour passed. Away to the left the outline of Plaza's guarding butte became faintly visible and as they coursed ahead a distant glow winked and wavered. To the right, some distance from the town a line of lights ranged slowly across the earth. Joe pointed the posse between these separate beacons, reached the road at a distance of around two miles from Plaza, and came to a halt. The line of light crept slowly toward him and the hollow rumble of the freighters grew from a remote echo to a confusion of noises — the same freighters that had left Smoky River at seven in the evening.

"What's the name of that wagon boss?" inquired Joe.

"Kearwill," murmured the redhead. "He's the fellow that found Bonnick's body."

"A-huh. A sensible sort of man? Belong to one side or other of this quarrel?"

"Fine fellow. He's a company man and he keeps strictly out of politics. He can't afford to take any sides, not when he goes through both sections of country all the time."

"Well," pondered Joe, "if it takes two days and nights to make a round trip, when does the poor devil sleep?"

"They was an alternate wagon boss for the odd trip," explained the redhead, "but LeGore chased him out of the country for some reason last week. Kearwill's been doubling up till they get another man. But as for them muleskinners, I wouldn't lend a nickel to any of 'em. No skinner is human."

"All right, boys," decided Joe. "Spread along the road to cover that outfit. Prob'ly be no trouble, but we can't afford any shooting. This is the way we get into Plaza sight unseen."

"Well I'll be damned," grunted one of the party, "if that ain't a neat idea."

The posse scattered to both sides of the road and stretched out to encircle the freighters. Joe, accompanied by the redhead and a half dozen others, moved quietly forward until the lead skinner, seeing the obstruction, stopped. Immediately, a horseman came galloping to the front. It was Kearwill.

"What's the trouble here?"

"Good evening," drawled Joe, suave and courteous. "Sorry to bother you."

Kearwill reached down to get the lantern from the foremost freighter. He lifted it between himself and Joe's party.

"Good evening. What's Smoky River doing out here? I smell something, gentlemen." He studied Joe more closely. "Where have I seen you before?"

"Night Foshay was killed, in Smoky. I guess this is going to interrupt your business, for which I sure am sorry, but I can't help it. Got to borrow a ride into Plaza for my crowd."

If Kearwill was a pleasant man he also was a firm one.

"Now, listen, friend, you're asking me to

take sides. I can't do that. It will put me in a jackpot with Plaza. My company has to keep on the good side of everybody. Fair play and fifty-fifty all around. I can't do it."

"Like Plaza, do you?" suggested Joe evenly.

Kearwill shrugged his shoulders.

"Personal opinion hasn't got anything to do with my job. I've got to like Plaza. It takes a diplomat to get along with those people. I have been walking on eggs for a year. If I help you, it will be my last trip through that town."

"As long as LeGore runs it," amended Joe.

"I see no probability of any change in rule," was Kearwill's dry answer.

"Going to be one tonight. Sorry, Kearwill, but I've got to do it."

"Damned if you are," said Kearwill. It was a flat and stubborn denial, yet without personal anger.

"Look around you," drawled Joe. "Fifty men in this party. They cover your wagons."

Kearwill looked. His face, worn from double duty and scant sleep, settled wearily. "I can't use force, friend. But you are doing me a personal injury. Remember that."

"No," contradicted Joe. "You will not be troubled again."

Kearwill lifted one hand in resignation. "Take it over."

Joe called softly to the posse. "Bring the skinners up here. Red, you leave five men with the horses. They'll take care of the skinners also."

Ten slack and taciturn figures came ambling up to the head of the column, herded by the possemen. The red-haired youth pointed out those men of Smoky River who were to remain behind. Joe rode down the line of wagons, inspecting them. "About eight of you boys climb into that first wagon, under the canvas. If you've got to pile out some of the freight to do it, go ahead. I'll be responsible for that, Kearwill. The next five wagons will take two men apiece, one to drive and one to hide. Ten and eight are eighteen. That leaves the rest of us to crowd in the last two wagons. Get going.

"Now I want the lead wagon to stop by the stable and the rest of them to string out along the street so that the last two will be about opposite the big saloon and the jail adjoining. When we come to a full stop, everybody pile out. Front bunch into the stable and cover whatever of LeGore's party comes back from the rear end of town. You gents in the middle wagons are to take shelter along the street where you can find it and cover anything that comes your way. The rest of us will smash into the jail and the big saloon. That's the hangout of LeGore's bunch. And we'll also cover anybody running back from the west end of the street. Keep together, don't go at it single. Watch the alleys. Don't put yourself in front of any lights. You boys driving will have to pull your hats pretty low when we crawl into this den of iniquity, for there'll be somebody posted to watch for trouble. But it's dark and they won't see the change in style. Hustle it. Turn those lantern wicks away down."

"How about me?" demanded Kearwill.

"I'd like you to ride ahead in front of the wagons just like business was as usual. When we stop, cut out of the picture."

"Is that a command or a personal request?"

Joe shook his head. "It ain't my place to command you, Kearwill. Figure it for yourself. Our gain tonight is your gain as well."

Kearwill relapsed into deep study. The men of the posse were crowding themselves beneath the tarpaulins. Kearwill finally lifted his head. "Think you can whip LeGore?"

"We smash his gang, we break his power. That's certain, once we get into town without being discovered. I mean to stand up to LeGore and see what the result is. I don't promise to walk away from that fight, but it don't make much difference. If he gets out of Plaza alive, he'll never dare lift his head in the country. Dead or alive, he'll be through."

Kearwill put out his hand. "It's been some long time since I've seen a man with guts enough to brace LeGore. I'm for you. Let's go."

Joe called down the road. "All set?"

"All set."

"Lead away, then." He dismounted, gave his pony to the Smoky River men who were remaining behind and issued a last warning. "Don't let these skinners get restless. No gun firing. Stick right here until you hear hell break loose in Plaza. Then come on with the horses, and get in the scrap." When the rear wagon rolled past he crawled inside the tarpaulin. Ten men had unloaded the freight from the vehicle and crouched down uncomfortably along the hard bed. Two or three boxes had been left on the tailgate as a subterfuge. Joe lifted the end of the tarp again to let in the air and watch the road behind. Thus at a snail's pace they crept nearer Plaza.

"I hope," rumbled a sepulchral voice, "nobody sneezes when we pass LeGore's nighthawks."

"Yeah," interposed another, "you would

hafta go and put that in somebody's head, wouldn't you?"

Joe lowered the tarp. "Easy, boys. We ain't so far away now and there's no telling how spread out the Plaza bunch is. I — "

A rider swooped down the line, circled the end wagon and drew abreast the team. "Hey, there, skinner — how about a cake of eatin' tobacco."

The Smoky River driver, secure in the blackness of the night, rose admirably to the occasion. "What the hell — I ain't no floating commissary."

"You can break open some of that freight, can't you?"

"Ain't got a thing on this trip but canary cages, brother. Canary cages and gold fish bowls."

"I wouldn't get so hard about it. Seen anybody along the road?"

"Some bunch of night owls passed across the road a spell back."

"Who was they?"

"Didn't stop to tell," drawled the driver. "Seemed in a hurry."

"I got a dam' good idea," snapped the horseman and spurred on ahead.

Of a sudden the train came to a halt and Joe, cramped between boxes, felt a fine cold sweat pricking his skin. Then they moved forward, rattling into deeper ruts. A light glowed against the tarp; through a small aperture Joe saw a pair of horsemen swing out of the roadside and follow casually talking between themselves. Corrals appeared, houses began to troop beside the highway; a watering trough gurgled and then they were within Plaza, and an occasional patch of light crossed the street.

Another moment and they would be abreast of LeGore's quarters, another moment and the sleepy stillness of the morning's small hours would be shattered with the crash and roar of factions locked together. Joe's hand dropped to his gun and he wondered if LeGore had suspected this possible use of the freighters; the horsemen still followed, though they had dropped a little farther back and seemed uninterested in the procession. Otherwise the street was deserted.

Up ahead, a Smoky River skinner began swearing at the mules in a loud, angry singsong. A whip snapped. Joe took hold of the tarp's edge, his fingers clamping into it with a terrific nervous energy. A brake block groaned against a wheel, iron rods clattered. The end wagon veered a little and came to a full halt; and with one mighty sweep of his arm, Joe tore the tarp away from the vehicle's rear, kicked the boxes down into the dust and jumped free with Smoky River men pushing him onward as they leaped. At the head of the column, a gunshot seemed to fill the town with its roaring. The riders who had followed the train in swerved from the middle of the street and swept down, firing as they came. Joe sent one plunging bullet at the nearest and never knew whether or not he had killed the man, for his ears were hammered with the crack of guns to either side of him, and under that savage hail both Plaza men swung out and down into the eddying dust like mealsacks. The town was swirling and spilling over with fury.

Joe raced for the door of the jail office, but it was blocked with figures of his own men fighting in. Once free of the wagons they had gone mad and nothing he said now would sway them. He had whipped them up and brought them here; the fight was theirs. They ripped the doors off the hinges of the saloon adjoining, smashed down the windows and poured through while a vast crying of rage and pain swept back along the path they made, mingled with the stench of powder.

LeGore had not been fool enough to place all his reliance on Cash Cairn's story; this town was pitted with renegades, each at some strategic spot. They were above the street, they were in around the corrals, they came spewing out of the alleys. LeGore had placed them well, yet the man, accustomed to seeing the freighters lumbering into town every day, had never thought of them as other than prosaic instruments of commerce. Because of that, the shrewd Breedlove had used these commonplace objects as machines of retribution. In a world of deceit and trickery, he had many times found that the obvious thing was the most deceptive.

Like a good general, he stood an instant by the side of a wagon, watching the renegades shift from the quiet areas into the very heart of battle, watching for LeGore to appear — and debating where he should look for Indigo. Resistance in the jail office had been crushed at one blow, and the Smoky River men were coming out of it and racing directly against a group of outlaws emerging from behind the corrals. Joe ran into the jail office, stumbling over the wreckage of desk and chair and odd furniture. One Smoky River man held a lamp over his head like a torch and pushed the muzzle of his gun at three sullen individuals against the wall. A fourth lay with his face down on the floor, motionless.

"We plastered this here bunch," grunted

the Smoky River adherent, "but I don't see why I got to ride herd on 'em. Let's put the brutes in the cell. Where is the cell, you sons of hell?"

A wailing, falsetto clamor came from behind a closed door. Joe, knowing that voice above all others, kicked the door open and looked into a short corridor on either side of which was an iron grating.

"Indigo!"

"Damn it, get me out of this damn' place before the fighting's done! I got some calling cards to deliver m'self! Lemme out, Joe!"

The tall partner turned to the prisoners. "Anybody know where the keys are?"

One of the men indicated the silent figure on the floor.

"He was marshal. He carries 'em. Left-hand coat pocket."

Joe knelt down while the Smoky River man holding the lamp broke into a solemn drone. "The wages of sin — "

"Shut up!" barked Indigo. "Nobody ain't collected no wages yet. Wait till I get outa here. If I don't make tramps of some of them lop-eared lulus — !"

Joe found the keys. He walked down the hall and released the little partner who sprang into the jail office like a madman, seized a captured gunbelt and wrapped it around his wasplike body as if he were trying to cut himself in two. His whiskers were three days old and the accumulated fighting urge made a pale green flame in his eyes. He stabbed the defeated Plaza trio with a baleful, glittering glance; he drew a mighty breath as if to sweep the cloying air of confinement from his pigeon chest, and out of his diminutive body poured a rebel yell that had all the nerve-racking effect of a charging tribe of Apaches.

"Come on, Joe! These slashing savages been wanting a bellyful of trouble some long time and now they sure are a-going to get it! Come on, Joe!" Head first, he dived through the office door into the dust-high, lead-swept street.

Joe tarried only long enough to watch the guarding Smoky River man push his charges into the cell and lock the door. "You're jailer," he said to the fellow. "Stick around, we'll have more pretty quick." Then he followed Indigo. Thirty seconds had scarcely elapsed, yet Indigo was crouched beside a freighter, shooting through the spokes of a wheel. Some Plaza cohort clung to the pool-deep darkness beneath the face of the butte and whipped the earth around the small partner with a headlong fire. Joe ran over to take a hand and felt a breath of wind fan his cheeks. A slug of lead smacked against the iron bracing of the wagon box and a second broke the ground at his feet. Swinging, his eyes lifted to the second story and saw an outlaw leaning from each of two windows. He swept them back with a brace of bullets, window glass jangling against the ledge, and he yelled at Indigo to follow as he galloped into the mouth of a street stairway. The little partner was instantly behind him, laboring with a released fury.

On up the stairs they raced and collided against a locked door; Joe's long arm hurled the impetuous Indigo away in time to miss a slug that splintered through the paneling. He braced his back to the far wall of the corridor and plunged a boot full against the door, tearing the lock through the wood. Powder belched at them, but they were veering aside and from the protected angles driving lead into the pitch-black vault. Indigo, at that summit of fighting madness where all sense of personal safety was lost, cried, "Now!" and pitched through the door. Joe lashed an angry oath at him and sprang across the sill.

The walls of the place shivered with the rending impact of that flaring, blind chance duel. It could last only the space of the revolving gun chambers, and when Joe heard his trigger drive home on an empty shell he dropped the weapon and shot his body across the space to the spot whence he had seen the last purple mushrooming of bullet light. A body passed the window's square outline; he swerved and crashed full against the man, driving him to the wall. He was grazed with a descending barrel, he was pounded in the vitals by a lifted knee, but his long arms gripped the unknown antagonist with the pressure of a herculean rage, jammed the man back to the wall again and in one mighty upheaval threw him full through the window, carrying away all that was left of glass and sash.

The room was empty save for himself. Indigo's opponent had ducked and fled with the little partner stumbling down the stairway in hot pursuit. Joe shuffled around for his gun on the floor, reloaded there in the sightless place, and took the stairs three at a time. The drive of every destructive instinct carried him along the street, seeking opposition. Yet all the personal combat he had so far passed through only served to inflame the grim desire to seek out LeGore and break for once and all the back of this bloody struggle. LeGore was responsible for death's riding tonight, LeGore's hand wrote this black page. Somewhere the renegade chief stood, nerveless and aloof, sending men to their utter doom and placing barriers between himself and Joe. The thing was monstrous, beyond every line of human decency.

He passed a man huddled in a dark doorway, sobbing out of a broken body; he looked into a saloon to see a group of the outlaw band standing, hands high, against the wall. Here and there individual combats were boiling up in the shadows, but the sudden and savage drive of Smoky River had swept the bulk of the outlaws into a knot within the stable where the slash and reverberation of the gunplay sang the strongest. This was their final stand, their ultimate bid for survival, and around them the men of Smoky River crouched and raced and shifted, seeking always for better avenues of attack. The echoes of struggle rolled down the stable's vault like a strong wind scouring through; dark figures moved in there, while from moment to moment more of the posse ran up from the other quarters and strengthened the cordon. Indigo was not to be seen. And where was LeGore?

Joe lifted his voice to the men of his party. "Save yourselves, boys. Don't get careless now. We've got that bunch corralled and we can take our time at it. No use framing up against the door to be knocked over.

Take cover and hold it. Few more of you had better run around to the entrance on the next street. They might figure to make a break."

A half dozen Smoky River adherents instantly shifted and disappeared into the alley. Joe followed and saw them diving for sheltered apertures across from the stable's rear door. Elsewhere, a Smoky River man had conceived the idea of blockade. He had found a small springbed wagon and now, pushing it hind end foremost, rolled it across the stable's exit. A rain of bullets tore up the side boards; the original-minded posseman yelled sardonically and vanished whence he had come.

Standing by the alley, Joe's attention struck here and there, trying to divine the mystery of LeGore's whereabouts. The drumming explosive fusillade had dropped to a more desultory pitch as if exhaustion had come over the combatants. Plaza was conquered and outlaw rule was near its death. As he realized the size of the victory and its tremendous consequences to the country he turned back toward the main street to stop the firing and call into the stable for a general surrender. He had not taken three steps when he heard a high and skirling whoop rocketing out of the Mexican quarters on the southern edge of town. That was Indigo's war cry, none other. The little bantam, always off on a tangent, had flung himself into the very bowels of the night and into a section no other Smoky River man had so far penetrated. Joe, swearing with a full heart, hauled himself around, recrossed the second street and ran on between the narrow confines of the alley.

"Indigo!"

His partner yelled again, whether in distress or excitement, Joe couldn't tell. He repeated his summons and halted where the alley straggled out to open desert, cluttered sheds and 'dobe huts. The area was without a solitary light and a queer silence cramped down. Even the straggling exchange of fire from the main street seemed a little muffled here and removed to a greater distance than it actually was. Then a door opened and slammed somewhere along the reaches of the alley, behind him. He threw himself flat against a wall and at that moment a deliberate, emotionless challenge rolled toward him.

"Breedlove."

The figure of the man was wholly lost in the opaque pall, but he would have known that voice among a thousand others. Nothing could ever blur the metallic, chestless monotone that slipped so evenly from LeGore's thin lips. All at once the heat of his anger subsided and a cold stream flowed along his spine. He heard himself speaking slowly, almost without inflection.

"I reckon it's a habit of yours, LeGore, to stand back and let other poor damned misguided fools get shot to ribbons for you. About ready to run away?"

LeGore brushed the direct question aside.

"I figured I'd have to hunt you down another day. It is God's gospel I would have followed you to the edge of the world. But I heard you a-hollering to that skinny little man and I knew the black ace had done turned face up on the table for you and me. It was in the deck. I ain't never before made the mistake of letting the wrong man cross my trail twice without taking him in. I made that mistake with you, Breedlove. You're the wrong man for me. I knew it when I set eyes on you the first time. I can tell. You're my kind of a man and two of them ain't never able to live in the same country together."

"Your judgment is plumb bad," murmured Joe, "in figuring us alike."

"It is gospel. You're on the right side of the fence, I'm on the other side. It don't make no difference. You and me has got the same bedrock. I never admitted another man was any harder than me and dam' few as hard. I am finding out about that point in the next minute."

"Hard?" drawled Joe. "If you're so tough, why slink around the back end of Plaza when my boys is shooting daylight out of your crowd. Hard, hell!"

"I know when my hand ain't strong enough," returned the invisible LeGore. "I knew it wasn't when you got through my guards. To hell with anything else. It's you I want. That's why I was waiting. I'd of worn the legs off my ponies looking for you. Damn your soul, you busted up my plans! You put guts in a pack of rats that didn't never dare lift a finger to me before! And I'll ride out of Plaza tonight with that settled!"

Joe picked up the soft shuffling of the renegade's feet; there was a slight abrasion of the man's body against the alley wall. Yet the tall partner stood rooted. "You have got a lot to answer for, LeGore. I wouldn't care to have that burden around my neck."

But LeGore was through with all explanations. His monotonous words came short and sudden. "Got a full gun, Breedlove?"

"Full enough."

"I am coming ahead."

Then the sound of the renegade ceased

utterly and nothing but a stifling suspense hung over the alley. The sides of this alley seemed to constrict until there was nothing but a tunnel down which the bullets must surely find him. If LeGore were advancing, he stepped with an uncanny quiet; if he were waiting, he possessed a superhuman power of self-control.

The moments lengthened until time merged with the ageless vault of the night and become nothing. How long he stood there he didn't know. His mind raced back and forth over every word and gesture of the outlaw and trailed oddly out to scenes along the distant course of his own life. He thought of the cabin sitting up in the canyon and the cool water lapping along the beach while the blue tendrils of dusk filtered in. That was peace, a remote peace that he never seemed able to attain. And the black alley held a tension that almost sang.

In those moments, heavy enough to sap the strength of a giant, he waited out LeGore. And broke LeGore. It was the renegade who smashed suspense, the purplish muzzle flame broaching the black screen somewhere half along the alley. The bullet's wash struck Joe's face. He moved forward and a second shot sliced the wood of the wall by him, breast high. LeGore's elevation was perfect and he was placing each bullet with a certain mathematical precision, from point to point. The alley was narrow and each slug, slicing at a tangent across it, covered a deadly range. Still Joe held his place and his fire. When LeGore's third shot sheered through the wall better than a yard or so in front of Joe, he at last drew his gun, stepped to the other side of the alley and came on, firing. He had six shells to LeGore's three, the range was point blank and from all that he could determine the outlaw was standing fast. He sent each bullet streaming along the wall, closely paralleling it, while the roar pounding against his ears nearly cut out the replying beat of LeGore's gun. But he saw the flashes gaping at him, first one and then a second. Closing in, he waited for that sixth shot. It never came. His hammer fell and clicked. He heard LeGore's body sag along the wall and he heard LeGore's breath come guttering out. Presently it stopped; the man's life was gone.

It seemed deathly quiet around Plaza. At first he thought his ears were bad, then he became conscious that all firing had ceased. Men were streaming down the alley toward him, challenging at each yard. He answered, feeling lethargy creep over him. Then he was surrounded by the Smoky River crowd and a lantern swung up and over a circle so that he had, for one short instant, the last view of Slash LeGore's gray, expressionless face staring upwards from the earth. He pushed his way clear of the party, hearing short, urgent orders among them. Orders to take up LeGore and move him out; orders to warn the Mexican quarter. He paid no attention to it.

When he got to the street the freighters were being driven out at a trot, men were running through the buildings and calling from upper windows. Already the Smoky River horses were in and being ridden; he saw his own and almost out of habit went over and stepped into the saddle. He saw half of the posse pushing the prisoners afoot, on westward from town. He saw the redhead and another party throwing the county records out of the jail office into a wagon and even while he watched the wagon pulled away, team at a gallop. Excitement seemed to pervade these fellows, strangely contradictory to his own letdown. Then Indigo appeared, also in the saddle, his homely cheeks relaxed from the fighting glower.

"Where you been?" grunted Joe. "Wasn't that you caterwauling back around the 'dobes?"

"I been everywhere," said Indigo, grinning.

His hands were shaking a little when he tried to roll a cigarette and there were violet marks along his shriveled skin. "Everywhere, Joe. And seen everything. I chased that Gilpin brute through every door and window in this joint. And — " snapping his lips together with inordinate satisfaction — "I got him. Yessir, I fought that gent until he just caved in. He's going home with the rest of them mugs to stand trial. The boys are right sensible about it. Not a one of 'em talking about lynching. They've had a bellyful of this business and they're blamed near peaceable. Yeah."

"I wonder how many we've lost," muttered Joe, sadness touching his face.

"I think two," grunted Indigo. He shook his head. "Well, what's that compared to the job done? We ain't ever going to know how much we've saved in the future." He gave up trying to roll the cigarette and sighed. "We done a good job and I ain't ashamed to say I've had a-plenty. You got LeGore, uh?"

Joe only nodded. Indigo cast a half glance at his partner and said gruffly, "It's dam' high time we was cutting this out. You might've got hurt. What the hell would I be doing without a pardner? They're hard to get nowadays."

Kearwill, the riding boss, came by and

reined in. He studied Joe for a rather long interval. Finally he put out his hand and gripped the tall partner. "I am proud to know you, Breedlove. That goes as it lays." Without saying more he pulled the pony around and galloped away.

"Let's ride," said Joe. "I ain't as young as I used to be, Indigo. I'm tired. I feel like I want to sit in front of our cabin and watch the water running by. Just sit and watch it."

Together they rode on through the street and out to the end where many lanterns were bobbing and the bulk of the posse had now collected. The redhead stepped before Joe.

"We're waiting for you to lead out, Mr. Breedlove. It's your party."

But Joe shook his head, feeling all eyes on him. "You've got to wind up this business yourself, boys. I'm an old man. I'm going back to the hills and sleep. Settle it your own way. But just remember the time for vigilantes is over. You've done what you started to do. It ain't pleasant to think about, but what's to be is going to be."

"How about these buzzards?" asked another, pointing to the outlaws collected.

Joe ran his eyes over the group. "You know 'em better than I do. I'd take the toughest of the bunch back for trial, including

Gilpin and Cairns. The rest I'd turn loose and point for the nearest county line. You got their names. Make it plain: if they set foot in the country again they're dead. No danger that way. LeGore's gone and Plaza's back is busted. This outlaw bunch is done for all and good."

He started away, then halted to look at them again. "What was you boys clearing out the town so quick for? Not intending to start a bonfire?"

The redhead looked a little sheepish. Joe shook his head. The weary frame straightened and the lantern light played full on the lean, kindly face. So he stood before them, blue eyes infinitely sad and the crusted silver shining below the tipped hat brim — a full and complete man.

"I'd think that over, boys. I wouldn't do it. That is somebody's property you're bent on destroying. So far we haven't done a thing we will ever be ashamed for. Don't step over the line. Let Plaza live, and its decent folks run it. So long."

A round, echoing "So long!" came back to him as he lined out across the desert with Indigo by his side; and in complete silence they journeyed onward in the paling shadows toward the hills and the little cabin by the river.

Ernest Haycox during his lifetime was considered the dean among authors of Western fiction. When the Western Writers of America was first organized in 1953, what became the Golden Spur Award for outstanding achievement in writing Western fiction was first going to be called the "Erny" in homage to Haycox. He was born in Portland, Oregon and, while still an undergraduate at the University of Oregon in Eugene, sold his first short story to the OVERLAND MONTHLY. His name soon became established in all the leading pulp magazines of the day, including Street and Smith's WESTERN STORY MAGAZINE and Doubleday's WEST MAGAZINE. His first novel, FREE GRASS, was published in book form in 1929. In 1931 he broke into the pages of COLLIER'S and from that time on was regularly featured in this magazine, either with a short story or a serial that was later published as a novel. In the 1940s his serials began appearing in THE SATURDAY EVENING POST and it was there that modern classics such as BUGLES IN THE AFTERNOON (1944) and CANYON PASSAGE (1945) were first published. Both of these novels were also made into major motion pictures although, perhaps, the film most loved and remembered is STAGECOACH (United Artists, 1939) directed by John Ford and starring John Wayne, based on Haycox's short story "Stage to Lordsburg." No history of the Western story in the 20th Century would be possible without reference to Haycox's fiction and his tremendous influence on other writers of stature, such as Peter Dawson, Norman A. Fox, Wayne D. Overholser, and Luke Short, among many. During his last years, before his premature death from abdominal carcinoma, he set himself the task of writing historical fiction which he felt would provide a fitting legacy and the consummation of his life's work. He almost always has an involving story to tell and one in which there is something not so readily definable that raises it above its time, an image possibly, a turn of phrase, or even a sensation, the smell of dust after rain or the solitude of an Arizona night. Haycox was an author whose Western fiction has made an abiding contribution to world literature.